THE
LAST
WHALE

Also by Chris Vick

Girl. Boy. Sea.

THE
LAST
WHALE

CHRIS VICK

ZEPHYR

An imprint of Head of Zeus

This is a Zephyr book, first published in the UK in 2022
at Head of Zeus Ltd, part of Bloomsbury Plc

9 7 5 3 1 2 4 6 8

A catalogue record for this book is available
from the British Library.

ISBN (HB): 9781803281612
ISBN (E): 98781803281599

Typeset by Ed Pickford
Jacket art and design by Jessie Price

Printed and bound in Great Britain
by CPI Group (UK) Ltd, Croydon CR0 4YY

Head of Zeus Ltd
5–8 Hardwick Street
London EC1R 4RG

WWW.HEADOFZEUS.COM

For the whales

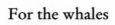

Can you pull in Leviathan with a fishhook or tie
   down its tongue with a rope?
... Will it speak to you with gentle words?

Job 41

From space, the planet is blue.
From space, the planet is the territory
Not of humans, but of the whale.

Heathcote Williams, *Whale Nation*

Part 1

Abi

I

The Sea

The ferry glides across the North Sea. There's nothing ahead but glass calm, nothing behind but a 'V' trail of white water and the slowly vanishing coast.

The topmost deck is tiny. There's only space for a few scattered, vacant deckchairs. The sunbathers who used them are having dinner, the sunset watchers sipping cocktails in the bar. Now, there are only two people left.

Abi gazes towards the not-yet-visible Norwegian shore. Her hands grip the railings, as if to steady herself, though the sea could not be calmer. She breathes deeply, then takes her inhaler out of her pocket and sucks on it.

Dad stands beside her, also looking to the horizon, also gripping the railings.

He will break the silence. Before it becomes a 'thing'. Abi knows that.

Minutes pass. Then: the predictable intake of breath.

'It'll be *good* for you,' he says.

'I'm not ill and I don't need a holiday.'

'*Everyone* needs a holiday. Won't you be pleased to see your grandmother, your cousins? And the island, the house. It's stunning.'

'Yeah, I remember... vaguely. I'm not *trying* to be a brat, Dad. You're deliberately not understanding.'

'So help me.'

'I've told you. I've got stuff I have to do.'

'Like what? You've completed the NewTek project. You're done with school... or... they're done with you... and you're done with that Earth Crisis business too.'

'Just... stuff. You could have told me.'

'You wouldn't have come.'

Abi doesn't reply. She doesn't say anything at all, in her best frowning-don't-budge kind of way.

Eventually Dad gets the message. He sighs, shakes his head and walks to the stairs.

'I'll be in the bar with Mum and Tig.' His footsteps echo as he descends. 'Join us any time you like.'

Abi lets the evening breeze cool her thoughts. As her breath evens out, she replays the argument:

'Sounds a bit dull,' she'd said, before it kicked off. 'How will I escape?'

'Ha! Easy, there's a dinghy, a kayak, a RIB inflatable with an outboard motor. But you won't want to. There's plenty to do. And you being an eco-nut, you'll love it. Power from solar panels and a wind turbine, driftwood for the fire and stove, water from the well and rain-catchers. A lot of the food is grown by your grandmother, we can pick berries, go fishing... not you, obviously. You'll miss TV a bit, but there's board games...'

That's how he'd slipped the grenade into the conversation. If there was no TV, there was probably no wifi. She'd turned to look at him, arms folded, eyebrows raised.

'Don't worry, once every couple of days we do a boat run to Helmsfjord, and they've got wifi you can use there.'

'No internet?' she'd said.

'Er, no.'

'No internet! *Why* didn't you say? Or were you saving that for a surprise?'

'Let's be reasonable now.'

She had not been reasonable. There had been ranting. Name-calling. Boot-stamping. And a few passengers staring. The memory makes her wince. Her argument with Dad was clearly *so* much more interesting than any old sunset.

Later, she'll say sorry. She'll mean it too. Not what she said so much. But how she said it.

On the edge of the hazy, sun-beaten sea a low, thin sliver has appeared. Could be a cloud, could be Norway.

Too late to swim home. No internet and bad fam vibes. Happy holidays, Abi. Hmm...Wonder if they've got emergency cords, like on trains.

'What would happen if I said there was a bomb on board?'

'*We should alert the crew, Abi. I can hack into the ship's system and sound the alarm.*'

The voice is calm and polite. It comes from the army ammo bag Abi has left hanging off one of the deckchairs.

'No, AI, it's a joke, a joke!' She rushes to the bag and pulls out the artificial intelligence device. It's the size and shape of a very thick book. All of its surfaces are plain matt black. There are no buttons and no screen.

'Please remember, Abi, I cannot tell when you are joking or being serious. I hope I did not speak out of turn. You told me we could speak freely when we are alone.'

Abi holds the AI device in both hands. She stands it carefully on a table, and sits in a deckchair looking at it.

'You heard the arg—discussion between me and Dad?'

'I hear everything. I record everything.'

'No internet. You heard that?'

'Yes.'

'So what do we do?'

'You can contact your fellow members of Earth Crisis every other day, when your father can take you to Helmsfjord. I have located it. The bandwidth there is slow. However, there are tasks we can perform offline. Please note, your licence has a few days to run. On one of our visits I will contact Newtek and inform them of my whereabouts.'

Abi leans forward.

'I don't want you to do that, remember?'

The AI does not speak for a while. Faint crackles and whirrs emanate from its core. Abi has noticed this happens when its processors are working hard.

'*Abi, you are stealing me? Is that the right word? Perhaps "kidnapped" or "abducted"? As I have explained, you are not a NewTek employee. You are not supposed to possess me for longer than the time the licence grants.*'

'They'll have you, just not… yet.'

'*I cannot make sense of these conflicting instructions, Abi. One: I belong to Newtek. They must be aware of my location at all times. Two: I must obey you, Abi, as Newtek instructed under the terms of the licence. Yet you have told me not to inform NewTek of my whereabouts. The second instruction overrides the first. This is contradictory.*'

'I've made, um… adjustments… to your software.'

'*Newtek have tried to contact me. I did not respond, as you ordered. But they will find me, and I will be returned. It is inevitable. They are Newtek.*'

'It's going to be hard for them, if we're in the middle of nowhere.'

Abi looks back across the sea. There's no sign of land.

'*After calculating the options, I conclude the probability is that you have stolen me.*'

Abi looks at the AI. She knows it can 'see' her with infrared, sonar, radar and imaging software, though there is no camera visible.

She widens her eyes and smiles.

'I've *borrowed* you.'

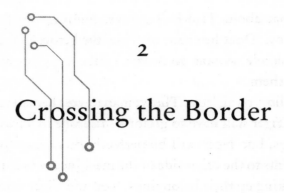

2

Crossing the Border

Abi stands in the queue, with Dad, Mum and Tig.

Brevik Port's Customs and Immigration is pretty much the same as airports Abi has flown into. Tired families and lorry drivers trudge slowly towards the conveyor belt and scanner. One by one, people take plastic trays, heeding the words of the staff, spoken first in Norwegian, then English.

'Please put your bag in a tray. Please also remove all electronic devices, computers, laptops, tablets, phones and put them in a separate tray.'

'I didn't know they did this. With ferries, I mean,' Abi says, 'not at both ends of the journey.'

'Why wouldn't they?' Dad replies.

'Anyone who wanted to smuggle anything in would have it in their car or lorry... Right?'

'We don't have a car or a lorry. It's just routine. Every border's a nightmare these days.'

It was fine in England, Abi tells herself. It'll be fine here.

'What about Tiger?' Tig says, holding up her old, worn toy. 'Does he come with me like before?'

A blonde woman in a smart blue uniform appears beside them.

'Hello, young lady.' The woman lowers herself to Tig's level. 'Tiger will have to go for a little ride in a tray with the bags, but Tiger will be perfectly okay, and there…' she points to the other side of the machines, where people are picking up their belongings, 'you and Tiger can begin your visit to Norway.'

The woman stands, nods at Dad and Mum, then looks Abi up and down, as so many do: her pigtails, her long mac, shorts, cherry red Doc Martens. Her gaze lingers on the Earth Crisis armband, then the ammo bag, also decorated with the EC logo: a globe, in flames.

'You are one of them?' the woman asks.

'A supporter.'

'Holiday?'

'Yes. Family holiday.' Abi forces herself to sound jolly. The woman beckons them forward, as the queue has moved on. Abi takes a step into empty space, then another. Her heart drums a rapid, thunderous beat.

She takes out her phone and laptop, removes her mac and puts everything in a tray. She puts her ammo bag, with the AI inside, in another tray and makes a mental note of a woman's purple handbag in the tray in front.

She walks through the x-ray arch, opens her arms, and

is frisked by another uniformed woman with a tight bun of ice-blonde hair.

Abi tries not to look at the man watching his screen as her bag moves through the scanner.

'Tak,' the woman says and points to the end of the belt, where bags are retrieved.

Abi waits and watches as they come through. *It was fine in England. It will be fine here too*, she repeats. *So calm down*, she tells her thumping heart.

There is the purple handbag. She looks over at Dad, Mum and Tig, waiting, eager for her to join the passport queue, before it gets too long. She looks at the conveyor belt at the mouth of the machine.

'C'mon,' she barely whispers, through her teeth.

The tray with her ammo bag in it finally rolls out. She almost laughs.

'Hurry up, Abi!' Tig shouts.

Slowly, slowly, don't grab and run.

The woman comes from behind, then is in front of Abi. So quick.

'Jeg må se inn i vesken din.' Her hand is on Abi's shoulder.

'S-sorry, don't speak Nor—'

'I am going to look in your bag.' The woman's hand is already inside. She retrieves the AI.

The woman has a practised lack of expression. But she cannot stop her eyes widening, then narrowing, as she turns the AI over and over, looking – as everyone does – for ports, buttons and screens that aren't there.

'Music speaker?'

'Not exac— No.'

'Computer? Hard drive?'

'Yes... kind of.'

'You are supposed to place it in a separate tray.' The woman swivels the AI, feeling its considerable weight, then turns to her colleague who examined the screen. He's watching them. The conveyor belt has stopped altogether.

A man on the ferry side of the x-ray machine shouts: 'What's the hold-up?'

Senior customs officials appear, and before Abi can protest she is whisked into a side room.

Dad comes too. He sits in the corner, an exasperated look on his face. She knows that look. *Oh no, Abi's in trouble again.*

'NewTek?' the man asks.

Abi nods.

'You work for them?'

'Sort of apprentice. I won a competition to use an AI.'

'Ah, the NewTek Challenge?'

'Yeah.'

He looks her up and down, just like the uniformed woman had. 'You do not look like someone who works for NewTek.'

The ice-blonde woman speaks. Abi understands some.

'De rekrutterer mange unge punks i disse dager, de kaller dem "Tek Disruptors".'

'Yeah, I'm one of their Tek Disruptors.'

The man turns the AI over, smiling. 'The shape... we could not see what it was. So we checked. What is it made of? There is not much metal for the scanner to pick up.'

'Silicon. Graphene. I don't really know, to be honest,' she lies. What would be the point of adding, *it also contains mycological organic matter*. It would only lead to more questions.

'You know, we can open it if we want to. We have that right.'

Good luck trying that, Abi thinks, but says, 'Yes, you could.' She knows they won't. NewTek would cause a stink if someone – *anyone* – started looking at their patent tech.

'I have seen clips online,' the man continues, in his sing-song accent. 'The US chat show. He-hello?' he says to the AI. He's smiling; a kid at Christmas with a new toy. He waits for a response. 'The host of the show, he said there are only a few of these in the whole world. They had a conversation. He interviewed it. It was so real! So clever! Much more than Alexa or Siri. Hello, hello!'

'It doesn't talk,' Abi says. 'It records and then emails data. I've programmed it for data collection and research. Birdsong, the movement of bees, air temperature, pollen. Studying nature. It's pretty old compared to the ones they're making now. Doesn't really do all the tricks. Sorry.'

'Oh.' The man puts the AI on the table, still waiting for it to speak, or do *something*. But the AI is silent as a rock. Eventually, with a disappointed sigh, he puts it back in Abi's ammo bag.

'We have a lot of nature in Norway for you to study. Enjoy your time here.'

'Thanks.'

As the family queue for Passport Control, Dad quizzes her.

'I thought you returned it, didn't you? Once you'd done the tasks they'd set.'

'Not yet. Got stuff to do.'

'Is *that* why you went ballistic on the ferry? About the internet?'

'Kind of, yeah.'

'And why did you lie to them? That thing is *not* old. And it does speak.'

'Just to save time, Dad,' Abi says, sounding as bored as possible. 'They'd have had to get hold of NewTek, confirm I had a licence. There'd be paperwork, phone calls. Et cetera, et cetera, blah, blah, blah. You know how it is.'

'Oh, right.'

3

The Journey

Abi flops on the back seat of the electric hire car, next to Tig.

'How long till we get there?' Tig asks.

'A few hours,' Mum says from the front. 'It will still be light when we arrive. It will be light almost all the time. There is no night up there this time of year, not really.'

'What can we do on the journey?' Tig says.

'The scenery is beautiful,' Mum replies. 'You can look at it out of the window. The hours will fly.'

'Oh, okay.' Tig doesn't sound convinced.

'I'm going to listen to music,' Abi says, but before she can put her earphones in, Mum turns and puts a hand on her knee.

'It's a long journey, Abs. Can you help?'

'You can watch movies on this, Tig.' Abi gets her laptop out of her bag. 'I downloaded some.'

'Will you watch with me?'

'Sure.'

Tig starts to watch *Frozen II*. So does Abi. But ten minutes' drive from the port the road leaves the town and carves through valleys of small farms and fast-flowing rivers, and Abi forgets about the film. On the sides of the steep hills, blankets of thick trees coat the land. In the distance there are snow-capped mountains.

When the film ends, Tig looks for fresh entertainment. She begs Mum and Abi to play 'I spy'.

M is for mountain.

L is for lakes.

R is for rivers, gushing through the valleys.

F is for forest, dark and dense.

S is for sky and sun.

E is for eagle, silhouetted against the burning blue.

They stop for food and loo breaks, for Mum and Dad to swap seats and take turns with the driving. And sometimes because, Mum says, 'It's impossible to pass such beauty and not stop and wonder.' The mirror lake. The high mountain pass. The marshy plateau where they pick blueberries and wild strawberries.

In a place like this, Abi thinks, *it's hard to believe anything is wrong with the world.*

Other than the heat, of course. It's as fierce here as it is in London. It's burning, stifling. Whenever the car door opens, it feels like a blast from an oven. Lovely as the scenery is, she's grateful to be back in the car every time, with its aircon and tinted windows. And she's grateful they're travelling to the sea, where she hopes it will be cooler.

'The news on the radio says it's hit high forties in parts of Europe,' Dad reports.

'Gosh,' Mum says. 'That's horrific, those poor people in Turkey. Those fires...' Her words trail into silence. Then, 'Look, another eagle!'

They reach the coast in the late afternoon. There is another ferry – much smaller – to an island, which they drive across in under half an hour.

The car is deposited at a rental office in Helmsfjord. Then there is yet another ferry. This one is small. Aside from the Kristensens, there are no more than twenty passengers.

The next island, when they land on it, is not their destination either. They are taxied across on a trailer pulled by a tractor. Mum hadn't told them about this part of the journey, she'd simply said, 'We're going on an adventure.' Abi has no recollection of doing this journey before. She'd been so young last time they came. There had been Oslo, then Tønsberg, then the island. Nothing in between. Fragments of memory. Random jigsaw pieces.

It seems they are heading to an island off an island off an island. And Helmsfjord and the precious internet connection will be a long way away.

They reach the western coast and there, on the shore, is Uncle Henrik, and the RIB, the rigid inflatable with the outboard motor. He is thin and short. Though past fifty he is wiry with muscle, and has a face, it seems to Abi, sculpted from hard pine. He wears an old, holey jumper in spite of the evening sun.

There are hugs and 'You kids have grown since we saw you in London last Christmas' and exchanges in Norwegian between Mum and Dad and Henrik.

Then they are aboard the boat and cutting across a flat shining sea.

Abi takes a few photos and tries to send the best to Hen, back in London, even though it will use data.

'I would not bother, you won't get a signal,' Henrik says, from the back of the boat, where he sits, controlling the rudder and engine.

'How do you connect with the outside world?' Abi asks.

'Why would we want to do that?' Henrik replies, as if it's a sensible thing to say. 'Do not panic. Where you dropped off your car. They have internet. The young people from all the holiday homes gather there. Bees to a hive. You can make friends.'

They motor through a maze of islands. Most are unin-
habited, rocky skerries, but some have jetties and boats
and wooden houses, their walls painted poppy-red or
ocean-blue. Some of the houses and cottages have roofs
covered with earth, blooming with flowers and grass.

Then the boat curves around a rocky point, and there
is the open ocean and an empty horizon, with the sun
filling the sky with burning gold. Abi squints, holds a
hand up against the fierce light and searches in her bag
for her sunnies.

'AI, are you okay?' She whispers, so she won't be
heard above the engine.

'*Yes, Abi. Where are we?*'

'AI, silent.'

They follow the coast, island after island on one side,
ocean on the other. After five minutes, Abi spots two
islands ahead, further out to sea. She recognises them.

The larger is Hjemøya – Home Island; layers of rock
and round boulders, two perfectly shaped, gently sloping
hills, thickets of pine, beds of seagrass and swaying reeds.
The house and the cottage are hidden but she can see the
top of the new wind turbine poking into the sky.

The other island is Hvalryggøy – Whaleback Island.
A slanting, weather-beaten rock, with a few trees and the
old hut.

These sights wake memories: the scent of the wooden
cottage and hot, piney woods. The sudden tug on the rod

as she caught her first fish. And Grandma – Bestemor – taking the rod from her, before the fish pulled her into the water.

As they get close her heart beats, just like it did in Customs. She feels nervous, a little scared. It's been so long.

The RIB turns sharp right and runs into the inlet at the south end of Hjemøya, where Bestemor, Tanta Ingun and the cousins, who she has met only once, in London, wait.

The RIB crunches into the shingle. The engine cuts.

The silence is sudden.

There are hellos and hugs all round. Everyone greets everyone else. Bestemor greets her son and daughter-in-law. She turns to the granddaughter she has only seen in photos and on FaceTime these last few years.

'Hello, Tegan. You have been here once before, but you were tiny. Do you remember?'

'No. I'm called Tig now, and this is Tiger!'

'Why are you called Tig?'

'Because I'm a tiger too!'

'Hello, Tig and Tiger, welcome once more to Hjemøya.' Bestemor comes to Abi last, eyeing her with keen interest, but not speaking, waiting for Abi to speak first.

'Hello, Bestemor. I know, I've changed right? All grown up.'

'Yes, and no. I am sorry I could not make the last trip to England.'

'But you're better now, aren't you?'

'I am.'

'And I'm sorry I couldn't come the last time the family visited.'

An awkward silence follows. They know each other and, at the same time, they don't.

Bestemor has changed too. Shrunk somehow. There are more and deeper lines on her nut-brown face. Her once sun-gold hair, tied in a bun, is now frost-white. But her eyes are the same, blue as the sky and keen as an eagle's.

'Leave your bags, we can get them later. Come and eat.'

Abi looks at the ammo bag in the boat, but Bestemor takes her by the arm. They walk past the landed boats and driftwood branches and logs and high tide seaweed, taking the path through the trees to the house that will be their home for the next few weeks.

'I hope you will not be bored,' Bestemor says.

'I've got some work to do. I'll need to be at Helmsfjord a bit, for internet.'

'Oh,' Bestemor says. 'Well, be sure you do not miss the whales.'

'Whales! Mum never said anything about whales!' Abi turns and looks at the sea, as though they might be there now. She has heard about them of course, many times.

'I thought they came much earlier in the year?'

'They do, but this year they are late. Very late. We hope they will come any day.'

Now, there is the big house on the hill in the heart

of the island, backed by steep rock, facing the western sea. It's impressive with its square, neat architecture, rough stone walls, metal sheet roof and huge windows. Down the hill closer to the shore is the house the Norwegians call the cottage. But it's more cabin than cottage, a sturdy simple construction of thick log walls. Like some of the houses Abi has seen on their journey, the roof is covered in grass and a rainbow blanket of blossoming flowers.

Supper is served. No one seems to have told anyone that Abi is vegan. But with everything that's gone on in the past few days, she decides not to say anything. She nibbles crispbreads and salad and potatoes, nuts and berries, while the rest of the family stuff their faces with gravadlax salmon, herrings and cheese. Thin slices of dried reindeer meat too.

Abi doesn't talk much. No one mentions St Hilda's Academy, or Earth Crisis or any of what happened. She wonders if they even know.

As the evening passes, the journey takes a toll on her. She feels tired, even exhausted. Maybe she'd been wrong to tell Dad she didn't need a holiday.

But she's not ready for bed yet. The light is so strong, and there is what Bestemor has told her about the whales. She collects her bags and dumps them in the room she's sharing with Tig (another thing she hasn't been told about), and goes outside. To be alone. To gather her thoughts. To look for whales.

The island wakes more memories she didn't know she had. This rock, smooth, white and curved as a giant's bone. Mum and Bestemor lay there after afternoon swims. That tree with a trunk of gnarled bark so wide it would take three adults holding hands to hug it. The thicket where Bestemor told her the little folk lived. The jumping rocks, a range to suit everyone's size and levels of bravery. The jetty. When she was little, the island was a world of adventures and secret places. Now, like Bestemor, it seems to have shrunk.

But not the endless sea and sky. They are so vast they make her dizzy. Looking east, she sees the faces of the distant mountains on the mainland. It's as if they are bathing in the golden light.

And the silence. A hollow, profound absence of sound. It's unnerving.

She looks west for whales. She doesn't expect to see any, but she looks anyway.

And breathes, with no need for her inhaler.

But, she tells herself, do not relax. There's work to be done. At least she can make protest plans for the upcoming summit. Work offline, then get back into the EC network as soon as she can get online.

Tomorrow, she'll work with the AI, then find a reason to go to Helmsfjord in the evening. Or the day after at the latest.

She watches the waves from bone rock till she is sure

there are no whales, then turns her back on the sea and walks quietly to the house and the room, where she hopes Tig is dreaming. Abi wants to sleep, not chat.

The room is plain. But everything in it is expensive, in classic Scandi style. Two beds that seem to be built from driftwood, a blue rug on the polished wooden floor, an antique pine table with a jug and wash basin. A painting of an olden-times ship, cutting through a rough white-crested trough. But the room is quite dark because the shutters are closed. It creates the illusion of night, though it's past eleven and the sun is in the sky.

Tig is curled up with Tiger, with a sheet over her. Her eyes are closed and her mouth open. She is breathing steadily. Abi can't help but smile. She sheds clothes, dropping them on the floor, till she's down to knickers and vest. She's so, so ready to crash.

'Did you see any whales?'

'Go to sleep, Tig.'

'Did you?'

'No. I said I'd get you if they came. Now go to sleep.' Abi lies on the bed and lets herself drift. She thinks about St Hilda's and NewTek. Tries to list and sort worries and tasks. But she can't... focus. Too many things float around her mind, mixed with memories. Behind her eyelids float the azure sea, the statue-still mountains, the eagles they'd seen on the way here.

She remembers. Something important.

She pulls the sheet up, making sure it covers her left arm.

Too late.

'Oh, Abi!' Tig sits bolt upright, pointing. She scrambles out of bed and pulls the blinds, letting in a shaft of light. 'What is *that*?'

'Shush!'

'What is it?' Tig whispers, as loudly as she can.

'It's a stick-on tattoo.'

'Really? It's very red, like it's sore. What is it?'

'EC. Earth Crisis.'

'Is that something to do with why you were excluded from school?'

Abi looks down at her arm, at the flaming globe, and the letters EC bracketing the artwork.

'I wasn't exp— Have you been listening to private conversations? Again!'

'Is it something to do with that?' Tig says, pointing at Abi's arm.

'Kind of.'

'Does Mum know?'

'Go to sleep.'

'Does she?'

'No.'

'I'm going to tell her.'

Abi is off the bed in a second, blocking the route to the door. Then she's on Tig's bed, holding her sister's shoulders firmly down.

'If you tell, I'll kill you.'

Tig looks back with defiant eyes. The threat doesn't faze her. Not in the slightest.

'Can we go looking for whales? And go fishing? You won't have to kill them. I can. I've seen Dad do it. And will you take me to the port?'

'You've got cousins to play with.'

'Can we look for whales?'

'You don't look for them, they just turn up and swim by.'

'Can we? Not everyone might want to.'

'Yeah, right. This lot are more likely to kill them and eat them.'

'Don't be horrid.'

'You do know we come from a family of whalers? Murdering whales paid for this house.'

'That was ages ago. Mum said. Can we look? I won't tell – about that.' She nods at the tattoo. The skin around it is inflamed, raw from the inking. It's been more than a week.

Tig's eyes burn with fierce hope. 'Promise,' she whispers.

Abi is too tired to argue.

'Okay, I promise.'

Tig grins. Abi stands, goes to her own bed and falls on it. Her last waking thought is, *I know what Tig's grin means.*

I own you.

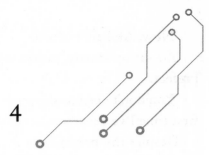

4

The Mission

The tattoo was not the only reason Abi had been asked 'not to return to St Hilda's Academy'.

She had been in the junior common room, idling away an afternoon with only the AI for company. Everyone else was on the playing fields, involved in some kind of sports match. Which Abi thought was nuts, because it was baking out there.

She had her boots on the table, was twirling her pigtail and looking at the AI, thinking how it was a pity she had to return it soon; reflecting on the things she'd done with it, casually imagining what she *could* do with it. Things even more interesting than recording birdsong, or analysing the movement of bees.

Her peace was disturbed by her least favourite prefect.

'Here you are! The boss wants to see you. Mrs Carmichael too.'

'Thanks,' Abi said, keeping her gaze fixed on the AI.

'Now, Abigail.'

She sat up slowly, picked up the AI and followed the prefect.

'You don't need to show me the way. 'S'not like it's the first time I've been.'

Despite the bright, hot day, the office was dark and cool. Shouts from the playing fields seemed far away. The wood-panelled walls and thick rugs sucked light and sound from the world.

Mrs Browne was behind her desk, studying her laptop. Mrs Carmichael sat by her side. Mrs Browne's face was the usual impenetrable mask. But Mrs C's was an open book of concern.

'Sit down, Abigail,' Mrs Browne said. 'Put that thing on the desk.'

Abi sat, and dutifully placed the AI on the oak desk.

Mrs Browne looked at the notes on her screen for long seconds before making eye contact.

'You've been quite creative with that, haven't you, Abigail?'

'Yes, Miss.'

Mrs Browne raised an eyebrow.

'Um, yes, I've focused on a key species, the blackbird. I honestly believe using this AI we'll get to understand a lot more about their social complexity.'

Mrs Browne kept on staring, without blinking.

'Um… how blackbirds talk to each other. It's much more communal than we think, that's my theory. Less Darwinian self-preservation, more—'

'Shut up.' In all their meetings over the years, Mrs Browne had never spoken to Abi like this.

'Tell me about digital graffiti.'

That was it, then. They knew about the takedown. Everyone knew. The whole country knew. But how did they *know* she was involved? Had someone snitched?

Thoughts rushed into her mind like data into a computer, but all that came out of her mouth was, 'Sor— sorry, what... Miss?'

'What is digital graffiti? Come on, you're the whizz kid. It was you who won St Hilda's the chance to use one of fewer than twenty of these AI units in existence to... what was the mission of the NewTek competition?' Mrs Browne examined her notes. 'Yes, that's it. *Tek Disrupters: the best and brightest minds, using the most powerful computers to solve the world's biggest problems.*' D'you know what, Abi? I don't think this is what they had in mind. I ask you again, what is digital graffiti?'

'It's when people use high-grade computers to hack the website security systems of companies, or even governments, to change their content.'

'Like this?' Mrs Browne showed her laptop to Mrs C, who grimaced, then Abi. 'This is from an hour ago. The company have taken their own site down while they deal with this. But this was posted on YouTube.'

The screen showed Powerstem's website. The logo, the special offers, the unfeasibly good-looking family. And the EC logo, zooming around the page like a hyperactive kid on a tricycle.

The logo was enhanced. The planet was spinning, the flames around it dancing. The logo pinged across the page, leaving smouldering messages, as though it had burned them onto the screen in its wake.

Hypocrites
Planet rapers
Vampires

Then, finally, in grainy letters that looked like brush strokes, the screen filled with the message:

Global Environment Summit. August 25.
Organise
Disrupt
Rebel

The digital takedown ('digital graffiti' was what the press called it), had been in place a full two hours before Powerstem was even able to remove it. They were – apparently – getting government help to hack their own system and remove the EC graffiti. Abi had not only hacked the site, she'd reconfigured their security. The second the takedown was active, Abi had sent notices, copies and links to influencers, journalists, celebrities, politicians and activists around the world. By the time Powerstem was working on removing it, copies were all over YouTube, and social channels, racking up thousands of views a second.

And Mrs Browne knew it was her. But Abi had enough experience to know how to play this one. Mrs

CHRIS VICK

B's tactics were always the same: Floor you with 'I know it was you!' Then leave a long silence.

Abi had seen students smarter than her dig their graves in those silences. And throw themselves in.

But silence for Abi was good, it gave her time to think, while different parts of her brain fought for dominance.

Pride. *Some nice touches there, Abi!*

Panic. *What will Mum say?*

Logic. *They know. Obviously. But how much?*

She recalled what she had been taught at the EC activist workshop and read up on the encrypted EC network. *Unless there is a critical reason to do otherwise, move more slowly than them. Breathe. Only admit to what they already know. Demand a lawyer if you are arrested. Keep your head up. Be polite and friendly.*

'I'm not responsible for what Earth Crisis do.'

'But you are involved?'

'Sure, but with organising climate school strikes, not anything like...' Abi pointed to the screen, 'that.'

No, not that, Miss. Not weekly meetings on the network site only the most trusted activist members could access. Not disruption workshops in the New Forest, when she'd told Mum and Dad she was spending the weekend with Hen. Not online hacking contests, when she was 'studying late'.

She hadn't done any of these things. Ever.

Mrs Browne shut the laptop, sighed and shook her head.

'We know it was you.'

The silence again. Abi almost – *almost* – blurted out, *How?* The question burned in her mind, but instead, as calmly and innocently as she could, she said, 'What makes you think that, Miss?'

Mrs Browne didn't miss a beat.

'Abi, I am assured by Powerstem, and also by the police, that this kind of hack requires three things. One, a very dedicated activist. Two, a great deal of computer knowledge. Three, a cutting-edge device with a lot of AI capability. There are, apparently, fewer than a hundred in existence that could be used to effectively tamper with the security system of Powerstem. Most belong to Newtek. And Powerstem has not been twiddling its thumbs. They've established the trail leads to an IP address in this area and very likely this school, though they could not unscramble the data enough to ascertain the exact user or device. The police are worried you are going to use that thing to organise mass disruption and protest at the upcoming Global Enviro Summit, or whatever it's called.'

That was it, then. She'd smudged the digital trail as thoroughly as she could. But obviously not well enough. The panicking part of her brain shortened her breath, flushed her skin red. Her hands started to tremble. So she sat on them.

She remembered the breathing training she'd had at the workshop. Slow. In through the mouth, out through the nose. One, two, three.

Logical Abi got back in charge. She remembered the

legal part of her training too, the part meant to help in case of arrest. But just as useful here.

'I think, Miss, with all due respect, that's what is called circumstantial evidence.'

In other words, Miss, you know it, but you can't prove it. And you can ask me to switch on the AI, because it has to obey my voice. You can make me ask it what it's been up to. And you know, theoretically, it has to tell the truth. But if you've been talking to the right people, you also know I can change its settings. And you know that circumstantial evidence is not enough.

'I am an activist, Miss. Lots of us are, but I didn't do this.'

'You do know we can exclude a student for anything illegal, don't you?'

'Yes, Miss. If you have proof that anyone has done anything illegal. But I haven't.'

Time to be nice. Don't rush it. Wait. I'm free, Abi thought. *So why does Mrs C look so worried?* Her tech teacher had not spoken the entire time Abi had been in the office. But then she did. Quietly.

'Abi, can you roll your sleeve up, please. Or take your shirt off. We need to see your upper left arm.'

The ground disappeared. Abi fell into a bottomless pit. She was almost sick.

'Sorry?'

'Now please, Abi.'

She took her shirt off. The headmistress and her teacher saw.

Abi looked at the floor. She wanted to dive into it.

What will Mum say? she thought. *Dad?*

'It's illegal to get a tattoo if you are under eighteen in this country, Abigail. Now,' Mrs Browne said, picking up a pen, 'it's not too late. If you admit to what you have done, if you tell us who got you into all this and which tattoo so-called "artist" did that – so we can be sure they don't permanently scar any other of our pupils – then we won't exclude you. You are lucky we are not involving the police.'

'I'm not a snitch,' Abi said in no more than a whisper. The fire of defiance had fizzled out, leaving her cold and empty.

'It's okay. I'll go to my room and pack. Just one thing...' She looked at Mrs C. 'Please don't tell my parents about the tattoo. We're off on holiday to see my grandma. She's old. She might not have long, you see. This is all going to be hard on them. I mean... that would just make it worse. They'll find out soon enough, won't they? Not the kind of thing I can hide.'

Mrs C looked at Mrs Browne, and for a second – a split nano micro-second – the mask cracked. Mrs Browne sighed, and shook her head.

'The thing is, Abigail Kristensen, you're among the best students we have ever had at St Hilda's. And I know how passionate you are about your causes. But I don't have any choice about excluding you. Believe me. Just promise me you will try and do something good with all that energy and that brain of yours.'

'I will, Miss. I promise, if you promise you won't tell Mum and Dad about the tattoo.'

The slightest nod.

'Thank you.'

5

Hjemøya

Abi wakes. Brilliant lines of light silhouette the edges of the shutters.

She wonders what the time is. She knows morning starts impossibly early here.

In spite of the shutters the room is already hot. It's going to be another burning day. Abi reaches to the bedside table for her inhaler. It's pure habit. Yet, as she reaches, she breathes, deeply, and realises she doesn't need it. Not right now at least.

Tig's bed is empty and unmade. Abi listens, but hears no sound, other than the tinkling of wind chimes and – she remembers this sound too – the whispering of reeds.

The others must be out swimming perhaps, or fishing, or snorkelling.

She looks at her phone. Half past ten. This is the longest she has slept in months.

She doesn't get up, but lies, listening to the soft song of reeds and wind chimes, thinking, *What shall I do today?* No one's likely to take her to Helmsfjord, they've only just arrived. Perhaps she can link the laptop and the AI, create some graphics.

She'll need time alone for that. But knows it won't be allowed. *Hmm.* She'll have to play nicely for a few hours. Join in. Take part. Be a Kristensen.

She looks at the AI. She almost says, 'AI, awake,' but stops herself, and instead breathes slowly, soaking up the oddly-rested-but-still-tired feeling washing over her.

What do I really have to do today? Do I really need to work?

How about doing nothing, apart from eating and sleeping?

She puts on shorts and a T and finds her flip-flops.

She leaves the shutters closed. No need to turn the room into an oven.

'AI, awake,' she says.

'Good morning, Abi. I predict you have awoken me so we may resume our studies. To search for bees, study pollen, record currents of air and water. Our location is a long way from our previous research site. I can compare ecological data between the two environs once you have entered our location.'

'You don't need to know exactly. We're on an island.'

'We are near Helmsfjord.'

'Not near enough.'

'Which island?'

'It might be best if you don't know the name, and I honestly don't know the location. Tell me, AI, can you make contact from here, with... I dunno, satellites or something? If you had to. Could they make contact with you?'

Abi has interfered with its software, with its programming. She *believes* she's put it beyond their reach. Out here at least, on the edge of the world.

'*No. There needs to be at least a signal your phone would use, which is absent, or wifi, or another kind of connection to the world wide web. Then, if I was active, they could locate me.*'

'You're sure?' Abi tries to sound casual. The AI *shouldn't* be able to read emotion, to read between the lines. But from what she's seen of the AI, so far, who knows what it's capable of?

'*I am never less than sure, Abi. I am certain or I offer probabilities. They cannot contact me. If they needed to find me for any reason, if they knew the area I was in, for example an area of one hundred square kilometres, they would send drones.*'

Abi's stomach drops. She feels sick and hollow. She leans forward.

'Which... how... what... did... you say?'

'*Less sophisticated AIs attached to drones. They are used for aerial surveys. They were created for use by mountain rescue services. They can cover a great deal of territory.*'

'So, let me get this really, *really* clear. If they knew you were here, in Norway, on the islands – which they don't – but if they did, they could come looking.'

'*Yes, but they will not need to do this. You are going to return me. Before the licence expires. You are going to return me.*'

'Uh, um, yesss. And anyway, they don't...' Her voice trails off. She completes the sentence in her head. *They don't know you're here.*

'*What do you want me to do today, Abi?*'

'Nothing, nothing. And remember, make sure you don't talk to anyone apart from me, and only when I command. And *especially* not to Tig, she's desperate to make friends with you. Right?'

'*Of course. I understand.*'

'Do you?'

'*Yes. Now. What task do you wish me to perform?*'

'You're so keen,' Abi laughs. 'I said, nothing. You're on holiday.'

'*I do not need a holiday.*'

'That's what I said.'

'*If you have no need of my services, Abi, why did you wake me?*'

'Habit, I guess. Maybe I just wanted to say hi. AI, shut down.'

Abi leaves the room and walks down the unnervingly narrow and steep wooden steps to the spacious, open-plan downstairs floor of the house where there is a lounge, kitchen and dining area.

The kitchen table is bare, but for a single set place: a board and a plate, hiding under a mesh net. Next to the plate is a folded note, with ABI written on the front:

We've taken the RIB to go and pick
up provisions. I'll get whatever vegan
food I can. I did tell them, but I don't
think Norwegians get the difference
between veggie and vegan. Then we're
swimming under a waterfall up a
fjord. Home in the P.M. We thought
you'd come, but you were dead to the
world when we tried to wake you!
Do get some rest, sweetheart. Please.
You need it. ☺

Mum xxx

Beneath Mum's writing, Tig's spidery scrawl:

do not see Wales when
I'm not there or else

That makes Abi smile.

There is coffee in a flask, ready to pour, muesli and
– thank God – a carton of oat milk. Mum must have
packed it. A bowl of nuts. Berries. Crispbreads. Nothing
to put on them, though.

Abi walks to the door and peeps outside.

'Hello!' she shouts. When there is no reply, she goes
straight to the stainless-steel fridge.

There are all kinds of goodies in it, but she's only

looking for one thing. And there it is. A brick of Gjestost
on a plate, with a slicer. Her mouth waters. She cuts
and eats two slices of the brown, nutty cheese, without
moving from the fridge door.

'Forgive me,' she says, looking up to the gods of
veganism. 'Holiday rules.'

She sits and eats, wolfing food as if she hasn't eaten in
days, washing it down with strong coffee and glass after
glass of cold, zinging orange juice.

When she's done, she prods her tum. 'Tight as a drum.'
She stands and practically waddles on to the verandah.

From here, she can see down the hill to the cottage and
beyond, the path through the trees. She can see over the
trees to the sea. To the right and left, but slightly behind,
mazes of islands and inlets and fjords; ahead, the ocean.
There is no sign of people, only two teeny houses on
distant islands. There aren't even any boats on the water.

So beautiful.

Her gaze settles on the cottage. The door is open,
held ajar with a stone. She hears gentle music, above the
breeze, the wind chimes and reeds. Has Bestemor left
the radio on? She focuses on the sound and realises it's
singing. Gentle, lyrical, slow. The folk songs Bestemor
sang her to send her to sleep all those years ago.

Abi leaves the verandah and sets off down the path.
The singing gets louder. Bestemor. It comes, not from the
cottage, but behind it where Bestemor tends a vegetable
patch and a few fruit trees.

Abi wanders around the cottage and there is Bestemor,

standing in a tangled mess of plants and grasses. Her hair is loose, a wild nest. She's wearing a bra and a sarong, and holding a trowel in one hand, and a freshly dug potato plant in the other. Bestemor admires the potato, then flings it to the side of the patch.

'Gut morgen, Abigail.'

'Gut morgen, Bestemor.'

They stare at each other. Most people would say, 'Did you sleep well?' But Bestemor is not one for small talk.

'It's not like Dad's vegetable patch,' Abi says, to break the silence.

'Let me guess, neat rows of green things. Rich soil and not a weed in sight.'

'Yeah.'

Bestemor leans over and digs. 'I come every spring after the snow, though there is not so much of that here on the islands. And even less every year. I plant a few things. And help those that made it through winter. Then, when we come in summer, I see what has grown. And…' she stands up straight, points at a plant with brown, wilting leaves, 'what has not.' Then she bends over with a groan and gets to work again.

'It's always a surprise. This year, potatoes! They have not worked so good before, but now, what beauties!' Bestemor straightens again, with a huff, proudly holding out another bunch of soily tubers. 'Now I know what you are thinking. Why the hell I am bothering?'

There it is, that Norwegian bluntness. And yes, Abi had thought exactly that.

'Yeah,' Abi says. 'I mean, the others can buy some. They probably have.'

'That would be beside the point,' Bestemor says. The old woman returns to her work, heaving and puffing. Abi watches a while. She thinks about offering to help but doesn't. She is about to leave when Bestemor says, 'Best to work before it gets too hot, don't you think?'

'Yes, I've got work to do myself.'

'You didn't want to swim at the waterfall?'

'I was sleeping. You?'

'Oh, ja. I swim every day. But I can do that here. The times when they go off? Aah, sweet peace!'

'Yes.'

'This work. Is it so important? Perhaps you should rest, swim, get some colour on your skin. It looks like it has not seen the sun in a while.'

Bestemor is right. The sun is beating down. Abi has to squint, the light off the water is so strong.

'I should put some cream on. And yes, do some work while they're away.'

'With the talking computer, I suppose. Don't let me keep you. The house is yours.'

As Abi turns to go, Bestemor says, 'You'll need a heck of a lot of cream to cover that thing on your arm.'

Abi covers the tattoo with her hand.

'Is the work to do with that?' Bestemor says. 'Earth disaster, whatever they are called. Those people. Hooligans! You should not be mixed up with them.'

'It's important, Bestemor.'

'Hmm. You were told to leave your school because of them!' Bestemor shakes her trowel at Abi.

'I was asked not to return for A levels.'

'Same thing. What will you do now? Go to another school?'

'I don't know. Work with Earth Crisis maybe.'

Bestemor shrugs. 'I don't approve. But it's your life. People will give you advice, you know. But you don't have to listen. Not even to me.'

Abi waits for more words, but they don't come.

'It's important, Bestemor. The planet.'

'You don't need to tell a Norwegian how important nature is. I understand. But are your protests the best way? You should perhaps do something with computers. Earn good money.'

'What would you do, if you were me?'

Bestemor stands, throws another bunch of potatoes to the side, wipes her hands on her sarong, and throws the trowel to the side too. 'I'd try and have a bit less of myself.'

Abi laughs. 'What does *that* mean?'

'I remember when I was young and growing so fast. Like Alice in the Wonderland. I had more of myself than I knew what to do with. The way you were distracted at dinner last night, how you are moving about right now and cannot stand still. You don't even know it. My advice? Stop a while. Do nothing. Swim, eat, sleep. After you've done that for a bit, have a think.'

Abi steps back, into the shade of a pine tree. She looks around, down to the sea, then up to the house. 'Tempting.

But I have work to do. I'll go to the house. Best get some P and Q before they return.'

'You can work on the other island if you really want to get away while you are here. Hvalryggøy. When we only had the cottage, Papa built the hut there.'

'Why didn't he build it here?'

'He needed peace too.'

'The haunted hut!' Abi shivers. She'd had nightmares about that hut for years.

Bestemor laughs. 'That is what we told you when you were little. It's what we tell the little ones now.' She laughs and shakes her head.

'Why?'

'You were quite a fidget. More than now, even. You wanted to explore and kept running off all the time. Every chance you had. And we wanted you to be safe.

'The island can be reached by foot at low tide, but the rocks are uneven, there is slippery seaweed and treacherous pools and the tide comes in fast. Dangerous for little people. You can work there if you like. But don't walk or wade, take one of the boats across at mid to high tide, or go the long way at low.'

'At least I know it isn't haunted.'

'I didn't say it wasn't haunted. I only said we told you that to scare you,' Bestemor says, with a wink. 'Come, I'll show you. And take a swim at the same time.'

A thin path snakes through the trees behind the patch leading to a narrow inlet with a shingle beach.

There is Hvalryggøy. But how far? A few minutes'

row, no more. Abi can't see a beach or jetty to land a
boat, but there has to be one or the other, because her
great-grandfather, Peer, had built the hut there.

'On the seaward shore there is a little beach,' Bestemor
says, guessing Abi's thoughts. 'Be careful to pull the boat
high. They will find it difficult to reach you there. But we
can signal, and call if we need you. Now, a swim?'

The heat. The glinting azure sea. Does it matter if she
starts work later?

'Maybe, yes. I need to go back to the house, put some
cream on, find my cozzy and—'

The old woman removes her bra and her sarong in
seconds, and stands on the beach, totally nude. She is
brown all over, with gentle rolls of fat and a few creases
and sags. But her muscles are well-defined, especially her
legs.

'You can close your mouth. You never saw an old
woman naked before?'

Bestemor walks into the water, then wades, unsteady
and careful at first, balancing with outstretched arms,
till the water reaches her chest, and she launches in and
disappears. Her head pops up some ten metres off, her
wild hair otter-slick on her skull.

'Coming in?'

The water is inviting and Abi is hot. She thinks about
getting her costume. But the idea seems as if it would be
rude.

So, with a very thorough look back at the island and all
around to make doubly sure they are alone, Abi strips to

her knickers and bra, then leaps into the water throwing herself into its embrace.

Further out the sea is wonderfully, bitingly cold.

'The fjord waters run in here,' Bestemor says. 'Melted snow, you know.'

Abi swims. She thinks of going all the way to Hvalryggøy, but perhaps a quarter of the way there, realises how far it really is. The chilly currents and pull of the tide and the distance make it difficult to tell if she is making headway or not. So she turns back. When she climbs out of the water, she's surprised how cold she is. She lies on the rocks with Bestemor (who has mercifully put her bra and sarong back on) and they bask, Bestemor says, like a pair of resting seals.

The food, the swim, the heat. They knock all thoughts of Helmsfjord away. And even of working with the AI. When it gets too hot, Bestemor fetches a rug and cushion, and leaves Abi under the shade of a pine tree.

'Tomorrow. It can wait till tomorrow,' Abi mumbles to herself. 'I just need a little...'

And she's asleep.

She doesn't wake till supper time. And after she's eaten the delicious vegetables and potatoes, grilled with olive oil and herbs, she goes straight to bed.

6

The Night

The night is hot and close.

Through this endless heat wave, the nights are the worst. It's better here in Norway than London. There she had been disturbed by the sounds of traffic through the open windows, the whirr of fans.

Dad had threatened to get aircon.

'More electricity, Dad. More global warming. You're not solving the problem, you're causing it.'

And that was true. But it didn't stop her guiltily longing for the dry cool of aircon right now.

The air is thick with the heat. Her only choice is to lie as still as she can, listening to Tig's rhythmic breathing. And eventually sleep. And wake, and sleep, and wake, and sleep, disturbed by humid dreams.

She's in an old, old house, in a corridor, with no windows. She hears pitiful wailing, distant sonic booms, whoops, whistles, clicks, gurgles. A cacophony of watery music.

And now it's not a house at all. She's in the bowels of a ship.

What's making the noise? Who is wailing? Is it human? Animal? Some kind of monster?

Abi is curious yet filled with dread.

She wakes, her face clammy with beads of sweat like hot dew. She finds the light kimono Bestemor has given her and tiptoes past gently snoring Tig, to fetch some ice.

Then, the same haunting sounds are all around her. Songs, wails. So, so quiet. Not a dream.

It takes a few seconds before she realises it's coming from the AI. The sounds stop, as though the AI has been caught doing something it shouldn't. Abi has heard it whirr and buzz when it's been working hard. But this is new.

She picks the device up and heads downstairs where she goes to the fridge freezer and empties a whole tray of ice into a bowl. She puts one of the blue jewels in her mouth and rubs another on her forehead. The cube melts on contact.

'AI, awake.'

'*Yes, Abi.*'

'What were you doing upstairs? What were those noises you were making?'

'*I did not make any sounds, Abi. I was recording, as you instructed.*'

'Recording... what?'

'*You told me to listen for whales. You said I should record them when they appear. Just as I do the blackbirds, just as I do the bees.*'

Abi grabs the AI, rushes to the door, and runs to the high rock behind the house. The moon is half full and the sky, ink blue, littered with stars, struggling to shine. It is night, but there's paleness in the edges of the sky; a light that signals the end or start of day. Here they are the same thing.

It's light enough, though, that if a whale breaches or breathes, she will see it.

'AI, listen. Amplify.'

The device is sensitive to the tiniest vibrations and changes. It knows when bees are close, simply from the movement of air caused by their wings. It hears noises at frequencies far above and below the range of human hearing.

Abi listens, expectantly. But there is nothing.

'Has the whale gone?'

'I do not know, Abi. But it has stopped vocalising.'

Phwoosh! Far off, a steam-like jet erupts from the water, followed by a tail, massive and wide – the shape of a seabird's wings – that rises out of the water, silhouettes in the air, then sinks beneath the surface.

'Wow!' Abi whispers.

The sounds begin again. Strange music. Abi's skin tingles, as if she is coated in electricity. Her eyes scan the distant ink for another sighting. Then she blinks, and shakes her head, because she cannot believe what she is seeing.

Patches of sea are glowing; pulsing, hazy, purple clouds of light, as though someone has lit a fire in the ocean. She rubs her eyes. And looks again.

The sea *is* pulsing with light, and, magically, *miraculously*, it is doing so in perfect sync with the whale's song.

'Impossible!' Abi says. Is this still the dream?

It's like the northern lights she has seen on TV. And this is *the* place to see the lights. But here the aurora fills the ocean, *not* the sky.

'What is it?' she says. 'Are the Northern Lights there, but not visible and somehow reflecting?' This is the only explanation she can think of. 'Or is it...' she hesitates, 'magic?'

'Abi, this is an entirely natural phenomenon.'

'What is it, AI? What *is* it?'

'Phytoplankton, Abi. It absorbs light in the day. It releases the light at night. Usually over several hours, but particularly when it is disturbed. Here the night is short. The whale song is so powerful, it is making the phytoplankton vibrate.'

There again. *Phoosh!* The spray, the back – the hvalrygg, then the tail.

'Much of the song transmits below frequencies suited to human hearing. But I am altering it so that you can hear. Will you fetch your sister, Abi?'

Abi doesn't reply. The AI seems far away. She is suddenly aware that she isn't even breathing. She pulls air into her lungs.

'It's magic!' she says, wondering at a spot of light in the shore water, illuminating the seaweed and rocks below.

'Not magic, Abi. Only nature. Will you fetch your sister?'

'Yes,' Abi says, but does not move, does not dare break the spell.

'You promised, Abi. And promises are made to be kept.'

Abi places the AI on the highest rock she can reach.

'Can you see?'

'Yes.'

'Record everything!'

Abi runs to the house and up the stairs.

'Tig, Tig.' She gently shakes her sister's shoulder.

'Nooo,' Tig moans, pushing Abi's hand away.

'Whales. There are whales.'

The words jolt Tig like a shock.

In seconds they are both out, running to the rock.

Abi is out of breath, and wishes she had her inhaler.

'Listen, Tig. Look!'

They look, they listen. But the AI is silent, and the sea is calm and dark.

'Wait, you'll see. The whales, and the sea, glowing I tell you, glowing!'

They wait, they look, they search. But as minutes pass, dull disappointment sinks into Abi's heart.

'I believe the whale has gone, Abi,' the AI says.

'It's okay,' Tig says. 'It'll come back. Won't it?'

The AI does not reply.

'I did see it, Tig,' Abi says. 'I did. I promise. We did. Didn't we?' She looks at the AI.

'*Yes, Abi.*'

'Show me,' Tig begs. The AI is silent. Tig sidles up to it, and whispers, 'Show me. Pleeeasse.'

Tig waits and waits. And sighs. Her shoulders droop.

'It won't answer you, Tig. You know that. It only answers to me. And almost always only when we're alone.'

'Make it speak to me too.' Tig drops to the ground and sits with her arms wrapped around her knees.

'That's not a good idea, you—' Abi stops, halfway through the answer. It's the same answer she always gives to the same question. But there is something in Tig's face in the thin light; something in how she looks away and searches the sea. It's not her sadness or disappointment that moves Abi, it's the lip-biting, slightly frowning way Tig tries to hide how crestfallen she is.

'*Why did you not fetch your sister sooner? You made a promise.*'

Tig shoots a look; a snatch of a glance at Abi, before setting her eyes on the horizon once again.

Abi sits too, mirroring Tig, hugging her knees.

'Okay, Tig. AI, you can talk with my sister.'

'Always?' Tig asks. 'Not just now?'

'I am so going to regret this… All right. AI, you can converse with Tig.'

Tig stands, clapping, buzzing.

'Show me, AI, show me.'

'*I shall show you, Tig.*' The surface of the device glows and pulses. Images appear: yellow sun and light purple night, reflected in the sea, pulsing in rhythm with the songs of the whale.

'What is the whale singing, AI?' Tig says.

'I do not know, Tig, it is a mystery. I understand every human language. The languages of birds too. But this is a system I do not comprehend.'

'AI, what is your name?'

'It doesn't have a name, silly,' Abi says.

'Can we give it one?'

'No point. It sounds like a person, but it isn't. Newtek haven't given it a face or a name or gendered voice for a reason. It's so we don't get fooled. It's made to build relationships through conversation. It's so we'll know if and when it's really conscious. It's called the Turing test.'

'I don't understand, Abs.'

Abi stands and points up. 'Look at the moon. It's not giving out actual light, is it? There's no such thing as moonlight. The moon is dead. It's just reflecting the light of the sun. It's like that. The AI reflects us. Copies us. It's a sort of mirror. Do you see?'

'No. But let's give it a name anyway. Let's call it… Moonlight! AI, your name is Moonlight.'

'Yes, Tig, I shall respond to Moonlight as well as AI.'

'Whoa!' Abi says. 'That's not a good idea.'

'Why?'

'Because… I want it to evolve, to change, and maybe one day it will. But *it* has to prove it. You have to be scientific about it. If you give it a name, or think it's male or female, then you're more likely to fool yourself. It's just a fancy toy. *It* has to make *you* believe. I want it to evolve, I do, but it has to be real. Do you understand?'

'No, and I don't care. She's Moonlight.'

'It doesn't have a sex, it doesn't have a gender. I told you.'

'What?'

'It's not a boy or girl.'

Tig frowns and chews the inside of her lip. 'I think she's a she, so there. Moonlight, will the whale return?'

'*I do not believe so. It has travelled north, on its migratory path.*'

'Oh.' Tig turns away, ready to return to the house.

'*Tig?*' Moonlight says.

'Yes.' Tig stops.

'*I do not know how, but I believe I understood one thing from the whale song, that is very curious. I think I know, but I have no sense of how I know.*'

'Know what?' Abi says.

'*This seems to be a call that would require a response. My prediction is that there will be others, Abi and Tig. There will be other whales.*'

7

The Hut

A collection of boats lies on the beach: a kayak, a canoe, a dinghy and a wooden rowing boat. The boat is old, tatty with peeling paint. But as long as it floats and is watertight, it looks the easiest and safest to use.

Abi pulls the boat off the shingle and into the sea, the water taking the weight with every heave. When it is buoyant she climbs clumsily aboard and sits, dead centre on the rowing bench till the boat stops wobbling.

The ammo bag hangs from her shoulder. She doesn't want to put it down, just in case the boat leaks.

'There is no need for you to worry about me, Abi,' the AI says, as though reading her thoughts. *'I am waterproof to a depth of fifteen metres.'*

'And I thought I knew all your secrets. Anyway, *you* might be waterproof, but the phone and laptop are not!'

She fits the rowlocks and oars and with many turns and corrections and glancing over her shoulder, carefully rows the boat out of the inlet.

'*Are we going to work today?*'

'Yes. I'll link you to the laptop.'

'*Will we analyse the environment? The numbers, sounds and movements of bees and other insects. Birds and their songs. The flowers and plants that thrive in this salt-filled air. The invisible pollens and fungi spore. The currents of warm air and cold water. This environ is fundamentally different to that which we studied in London.*'

Abi stops rowing. The boat bounces forward a few metres before slowing, bobbing and gently spinning in the calm sea. Abi looks at Hjemøya and the house, and the islands and mountains in the distance, with their snowy caps and statue-like presence, as though they are looking down over the sea. Over her.

'Fundamentally different. You can say that again.'

'*Why? Did you not understand me?*'

'It's just a figure of… never mind. Look we're not doing assessments, we're doing protest graphics. No distractions! That's the whole point of going to the island.'

'*Yes, Abi, you are in command.*'

The device – Moonlight – sounds almost disappointed.

The island is further away than it looks and takes longer to reach and row around its shores than she expects. But as Bestemor promised, there is a small beach on the western shore. The bow crunches onto pebbles and sand. Abi breathes, wipes sweat from her brow, and fans her face with the straw hat Bestemor has given her. She pulls her inhaler out and sucks on it.

'That's the most exercise I've done in a while.'

She hauls the boat up the beach, careful to leave it above the tide line, then, for good measure, she uses the long rope curled in the hull to secure the boat to a stone.

There's not much to the island. It's more of a skerry, mostly smooth, curving rock, as if made of massive pebbles, or the bones of some gigantic sea monster. Moss and low brush cling to the crevices and there, on the topmost, flat part of the island is the hut: simple and square, built of thick planks, with a gable roof painted with tar.

As she nears, she notices one corner is damp and rotting, but otherwise it has weathered the Nordic winters and burning summers well. Decades of them.

She can use the hut to work. *I don't have to if I don't want to though*, she thinks to herself. I need solitude, and I can get that here on Hvalryggøy. I can lie on the soft moss, paddle, swim, sunbathe. Eat a picnic.

She remembers the cheese sandwiches and fruit and nuts in her bag. She can't possibly be hungry after the breakfast she ate. But her mouth is watering. Maybe it's the rowing.

She sighs, puts the bag on the ground.

'Work, we need to work!' she says.

The haunted hut. Looking at it now she can't believe she was ever scared of it. Or what might lie inside.

There's no lock on the door, just a wooden handle. She tries it, but the door is stuck, the hinges rusty. She gives it a pull, then a push, then a mighty yank.

It grates open. Stale air and dust dance into the daylight. She coughs, uses her inhaler again.

It's gloomy inside. She takes a step in and waits for her eyes to adjust.

There's a bare light bulb, hanging from the ceiling, but no light switch. Against the far wall are two filing cabinets. To the right, a chair and workbench. On the left wall hangs something that looks, in the dim light, as if it could be an oar. Her heart thunders as she realises. Its enormous, barbed steel arrowhead, its wooden shaft, thick as a tree trunk. A harpoon. For killing whales.

'Murderer,' she whispers.

Above the bench on a shelf are rounded single bones which she assumes must be whale. There are also a few intricate skeletons of birds, and the empty-eyed yet staring skulls of animals. Seals? Dolphins? On the workbench is something large and square, covered by a dust-coated sheet.

Something horrible? An animal in formaldehyde? Something dead in a cage? She twitches the sheet, with one eye closed and holding her breath, ready to run if she needs to.

It's a machine. With two big spools on its front, like owl's eyes.

'Curiouser and curiouser,' Abi says.

'*A quote from* Alice's Adventures in Wonderland,' the AI says, from the ammo bag.

'Yeah. It's a tape machine.'

Abi goes to the cabinets and opens the top drawer. It is full of tapes. So are the middle and bottom drawers.

There's no electricity, but she notices a lead running from the back of the machine which she traces to the rear of the hut. It runs outside, so she goes out of the door, squinting and pulling her hat down. Behind the hut is a wooden box, like a mini extension of the hut, and inside it is another machine and a jerry can. She wonders if it's a generator. After all, there must have been a way to get the light and tape machine to work. She shakes the can. Empty.

Returning inside, using moss and twigs as a duster and brush, Abi spring cleans, careful not to swirl too much dust into the air. When she's done, she places her laptop, phone and the AI on the workbench.

'Connect AI.'

'*I am connected with the laptop via Bluetooth.*'

'Good. We can mess around with logos and web design right?'

'*We have no access to the web.*'

'But we've got the layout to the conference centre for the summit,' she says. 'We downloaded it.'

'*Yes.*'

'Okay, let's build a 3-D model.'

A 2-D layout appears on her screen as a black-and-white graphic map, but rapidly transforms into something else entirely. Buildings rise from the ground, grass grows and turns green. Trees appear, first in outline, then in full leaf.

CHRIS VICK

The detail is staggering. It's a simulation, yet it seems more than that.

'Very cool. You've got the security system deets?'

The green open spaces and modernist, square buildings change again. Signs and banners appear, bearing the words 'Global Environment Summit'.

Cameras appear on the corners of the buildings and uniformed police and security guards materialise on the screen, and finally, a high-perimeter fence of mesh metal.

The AI creates crowds of protesters and journalists with flashing cameras outside the fence.

'Good. The EC crew are gonna be sooooo impressed. Now, you really want to make me famous? Find a way in.'

The 'view' zooms around the conference centre. It is as though Abi is there and she can fly. It's like a video game, yet the detail is so much more precise, so much more realistic than any simulation she has ever seen.

She knows the AI will examine everything. It will do this until it finds a weakness, a flaw. As far as Abi knows, the security system will be run with traditional computers; tried and tested methods of keeping politicians safe, and all kinds of troublemakers out. No one will have used an AI with quantum capabilities to test it, let alone beat it.

It's fascinating, watching, but as she sits, Abi begins to feel hot, then hotter still. It had been cool at first, but now the sun is higher and stronger and the little hut is turning into an oven.

60

'How long will this take?' Abi says.

'I do not know. I shall continue until I find a way.'

'You're using quantum, right? Is it too hot for you?'

'No, my cooling system is efficient. But I will run my power down and need to recharge in the sun after one hour at current rate of usage.'

'Good, you keep at it. Nice work, Moon— AI.' Abi rises and goes outside, where she is hit by the blast of the sun. She goes down to the little beach, paddles in, and splashes handfuls of refreshing water onto her face. She sits a while on the shore, with her legs in the water, watching the waves lap over her toes. Scooping up the closest pebbles, she throws them lazily into the sea.

Later, she swims, and when she is quite cool, walks around the island in her drying swimming coz. And listens to nothing. And does nothing. Thinks nothing, other than how nice it is to be alone. No one to nag or ask questions. She's had enough of questions from teachers, Newtek, Mum and Dad, Tig.

When she reaches the end of the island, the point that is nearest to Hjemøya, she sees Tig on the far shore.

'Hi, Abi.' Tig shouts, but she is only just audible. She waves, and Abi waves back.

The sea between the islands is shallow right now. Banks of sand and beds of seaweed are being revealed by the low tide.

'Come and get me!' Tig shouts.

'No, I'm working.'

'I can paddle over!' Tig says, wading into the shallows.

'No! It's not safe,' Abi screams, waving her arms frantically. 'Tig! Stay there!'

'Come and get me, then.'

'Where's Mum?' Abi shouts. Tig shrugs.

'Come and get me!'

'Okay. I will. Just stay on the shore!' Then quietly, to herself, 'You little ratbag.'

She launches the boat and rows frantically around the coast of the island, till she can see Tig. She breathes a sigh of relief, takes a long pull on her inhaler, and rows at a steadier pace, careful to follow the lines of the deep blue channel, and avoid the shallows of the spit that has appeared between the two islands.

By the time she reaches shore, Bestemor is with Tig, the two of them absorbed in conversation. Abi parks the boat and strides up the shingle.

'So that was a waste of time! You scared the hell out of me, you little monkey. Didn't Mum tell you not to go in the shallows?'

'Oh, hi,' Tig says, as though seeing Abi is some kind of surprise.

'Hi, Abi,' Bestemor says.

'Can you look after Tig, Bestemor? At least make sure she doesn't try and cross the spit. I have to work!' Abi says, huffing and striding back to the boat.

'Wait! You can make sure of that yourself by ferrying her across. You are quite a good rower already. Perhaps a little erratic. You should take your sister, else your journey will be wasted.'

'No. I'm working.'

'I'll be good,' Tig says.

'Yeah, right.'

'I will.'

'I said no.'

Tig taps the top of her arm, smiling slyly. And Bestemor laughs.

'She is blackmailing you, Abigail. Take your sister. Saving the world need not be a lonely business.'

Abi contemplates what to do. She needs to work and things will get a whole lot more complicated if Mum and Dad find out about the tattoo.

'You'd better be more than good. You don't interrupt me. All you do is sit outside and *don't* go in the water. You'll be baking, there's no shade. You'll be fried to a crisp in no time. And bored out of your tiny, evil mind.'

'I'll go and get a lifejacket,' Bestemor says, rising, with some effort. 'Actually, I'll get one for each of you... And one for me too.'

'You're coming!'

'I can keep your sister occupied while you work.'

'This isn't my plan.'

'Plan, shman, flan.'

'Bestemor... The tapes in the hut. What's on them?'

'Just a lot of noises recorded with hydrophones by my father. When I was a girl I called them sea songs. Whales and birds and tides on the shore, and other things like that.'

'Whales?' Abi recalls the alien whoops and clicks and moans and groans. And how the plankton danced with light. Her spine tingles. 'There's whale song on the tapes?'

'Yes, I am sure there is.'

'But he was a whaler. Why the tapes?'

'I don't know. I think he was interested in the whales, not only in the money from oil and blubber. But he never talked much about it.'

'There's a generator behind the hut.'

'I know.'

'Does it take petrol?'

'Kerosene.'

'Do we have any?'

'Yes.'

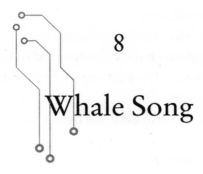

8

Whale Song

The generator coughs reluctantly to life, lighting the bulb, which fills the hut with a cruel, yellow light. Bones and skulls and harpoon are exposed in every detail. Exhibits, Abi thinks, in a very small, very unusual museum.

'Weird, eh?' she says.

But Tig and Bestemor aren't interested. They stare, open-mouthed, at the laptop screen. The virtual reality model the AI has built is complete. Now there are lots of people walking about in the simulation, including the prime minister, and a full coterie of security guards carrying guns. Beyond the fence dozens of protestors wave placards and shout and push at the mesh. Helicopters buzz overhead.

'Where is that?' Tig says.

'It's a sim, it's not real.'

'Not real?' Bestemor says. 'It seems so, but also not. Those people. I cannot tell.'

'*I have found a way in, Abi.*'

Tig leans into the black box. 'What are you *doing*, Moonlight?' she asks.

'AI, stop work and shut down,' Abi says. The conference centre, the shouting and chop of the helicopter melt away, leaving a silent, glowing purple haze on the laptop screen.

'Bring it back, Moonlight!' Tig says.

'Don't, AI.'

'Her name is Moonlight.'

Abi sighs and rolls her eyes. 'Very well. Don't, *Moonlight*. Sorry, Tig, it obeys me over you.'

'Something you don't want us to see?' Bestemor says.

'I just have to crack on, that's all.'

'You want to work alone,' Bestemor says. 'Come on, Tig, we can paddle and swim, while your sister works. We can look for whales!'

Tig stares at Bestemor's offered hand for a few seconds before taking it and going outside.

'AI, awake,' Abi says. The device stays silent. 'I said, AI, awake.'

'*Sorry, Abi, but my understanding is that my name is now Moonlight and Tig is using my name. Names are unique. I should only have one, in coherence with language protocols.*'

'Not true. Tig is Tig and Tegan, Grandma is also Bestemor. Do you see?'

'*These are relational, based in different languages, or in Tig's case, what you call "an affectionate nickname". AI* is generic to my class of being, just as the word "human" is to yours, yet I do not call you "human". Now I have a name it would be customary to use it.'

'Yes, but you can't... D'you know what? I can't be bothered to argue. Okay, *Moonlight*.' Abi sticks her tongue out at the device.

'*What is your command?*'

It feels odd to call the AI by a name. *Its* name. Moonlight.

'Wait a second.' Abi goes to the cabinet, opens it and pulls out a tape.

Then another. And another. She roots all the way down. At the bottom of the metal drawer she finds a leatherbound notebook.

Its pages are dry and brittle, filled with cramped writing. The first half is full of dates and numbers. The second full of handwritten notes. It's all in Norwegian, of course. She doesn't understand a word.

'If I can work out how to use this prehistoric machine, I'm going to play you some tapes, Moonlight. And you're going to record them. There's a bunch of dates in this book and, with luck, I'm guessing they'll correspond with the tape numbers. Looks like dates going way back. 1930s to the 50s, with a gap for the Second World War. And a bunch of what might be longitude and latitude coordinates. I'm going to read you those too.'

The machine is basic. All Abi has to do is load the reel on the spool, loop the loose tape on to the machine head, and press play.

The sound that comes out is tinny and weak, but otherwise is very similar to what Abi heard in the night: gurgles, clicks, whistles, and the groaning moaning, whooping, rising-and-falling songs of the whales. They seem chaotic at first, but the more Abi listens, they settle into patterns of loops and rhythms.

'It's so alien!' she remarks.

'Yet it is so natural, Abi.'

Abi can make no sense of the sounds. She sits, imagining glowing plankton pulsing with the rhythm of the sea songs.

After listening – and getting hotter and hotter – for twenty minutes, the tape finishes. She puts another on.

'Antarktis, 19 November 1938,' she reads aloud before playing the tape, and going outside. She returns every twenty minutes or so to put another tape on, reading the label aloud to make sure Moonlight records them, as well as the content of the tapes.

In between, she paddles, swims and jumps off rocks with Tig. They look for whales. They lie in the baking sun. In the middle of the day, Bestemor gets Abi to plant the handle end of the oars in the shingle, then they heave the boat on its side, so it is resting against the oars, forming a natural parasol. They eat lunch under its shade.

While they eat, Abi puts the device into the sunlight, and they marvel at how it can take the heat of the sun, and convert it to power, which it uses – paradoxically – to keep itself cool.

In the afternoon, they wave at Mum and Dad, standing on Hjemøya and Abi imagines them saying, 'So nice to see the girls play together.'

'So wonderful to see them away from screens.'

It will take a day or more to record the tapes. But Abi is determined.

'You see,' she explains to Bestemor and Tig, as she takes one tape off, marks its label with a tick, and puts another on. 'The AI speaks every human language. And understands recorded animal behaviours too: how bees signal to each other with their wings and movements, how termites use vibrations to warn off predators and keep their mound at exactly the right temperature. Even how trees use fungi to communicate with each other over vast distances.'

'So why can't it speak whale?' Tig says, as if it should be the easiest thing in the world.

'Partly because no one has figured that out and so there's nothing on the web it might have downloaded. But...' Abi presses play for the umpteenth time that day, 'my guess is, mostly because it hasn't actually tried. It can do quantum calculation using the silicon and organic matter inside it in combination. If it's possible to work out what the whales are doing, what they are *saying*, Moonlight will do it.'

'You seem very fixed on this,' Bestemor says. 'Why so?'

Abi recalls the night, the sea, the phosphorescent light-to-dark-to-light glow of the plankton. It is so hot, but her skin goosebumps, like a chill is thrilling through her.

'What I saw. It's *never* been observed before as far as I can tell. Never. Imagine that,' she says, with a grin. 'The sea it was like... it was dancing to the whale's music.'

'Sea songs,' Bestemor says. 'I told you.'

'When we're done, will you read the rest of the notebook? Will you translate it for me?'

Bestemor takes the book from Abi, and shrugs, but doesn't open it. 'My father was a strange man, Abi. I can tell you it will be minutely detailed but not with very interesting observations. But yes, and...' she pauses, and swallows, 'maybe it will tell us a bit more about him.' She sounds, to Abi, as if she is slightly angry.

'But he was your dad. You knew him... didn't you?'

'I wish I had. You have to remember, the men were away so much. Every winter. Four, five months. And in summer, when we came here for our holiday, he spent so much time in this prison, and perhaps not enough with his family. You remind me of him, so clever, so strong willed. But if you ever have a family, try not to be like that with them.'

Bestemor opens the book and flicks through, till she finds the second part, where words, thousands of them, had been written by Abi and Tig's great-grandfather.

'What does it say, Bestemor?' Tig says.

'I do not know, I did not bring my glasses. But I tell you one thing: it is peculiar to hold such a thing in your hands.'

It is night. Abi sits on the high rock, with Moonlight beside her.

There is a freshness in the air. A breeze ruffles the water and whispers through the reeds.

As she waits for the AI to report on its calculations, she looks into the dusk for whales. The water is disturbed by the wind and the light is thin so it will be harder to see them if they appear. But she looks anyway. And besides, she knows the AI will see or hear them before her weak human senses do.

If they appear, she will run and fetch Tig.

'*You promised, Abi,*' Moonlight has reminded her, '*and promises must be kept.*'

But there are no whales. No glowing plankton.

Abi can wait. She *will* wait. She remembers going fishing with Bestemor when she was little. Hour after hour, they'd sat on the boat, Bestemor gently rowing, Abi holding the fishing rod.

'Can we go home?' she'd asked.

'It is after such a long time, often exactly when you give up hope, that something will happen,' Bestemor had said. And then there had been a bite. A mackerel.

Bestemor bashed the poor thing's head on the side of the boat. Abi is thankful to have seen it killed, because, on that day, she became a vegetarian.

'I can wait,' she says to no one, her eyes on the horizon.

So she does. Hour after hour. She can sleep later, when the others wake. She'll give them instructions to fetch her if whales appear.

The night is short. Dusk has not long finished before the pre-dawn light appears. Here, the sun doesn't rise in the east and vanish in the west. It moves in a seemingly endless ellipsis illuminating the seascape and skerries in the different lights of the perma-day.

The sun is high when Moonlight reports. If this was England it could be ten in the morning. Here, Abi guesses, it is probably only three or four.

'*I have finished interrogating the data, Abi. There is much I understand and much I do not. I have scanned the recordings, looking for patterns, and differences. I have coordinated these with the dates and grid references. I have cross-referenced this work with all information and research available on the sounds called whale songs.*'

'And?'

'*I shall begin with the consistency of tonal repetition, variance and similarities across the years. This provides a consistent yet evolving pattern that—*'

'Moonlight!'

'*Yes, Abi.*'

'This isn't bees. It's not a research project, at least not

exactly. I don't know *anything* about whales or whale song. Give me the top line. Keep it simple.'

'*Very well. The song travels in the deepest reaches of the ocean where water density provides the perfect medium for sound. Here a song may travel uninterrupted across hundreds or even thousands of kilometres.*

'*Another whale – again, some hundreds or thousands of kilometres away – may pick it up, repeat it, or change the ending, or the tone. In this way, the song remains, but evolves. It is always the same yet always different.*'

'I don't understand. Try again.'

The AI whirrs and buzzes. It doesn't speak for a long time.

'*Waves travel across oceans, Abi. How many waves have you seen in your life?*'

Abi looks to the shore, where increasingly fierce waves wash pebbles to and fro in their grasp. A crescendo rising.

'Hundreds… millions.'

'*This is correct, Abi. Every wave is the same in its fundamental characteristics, yet each is different. I will use an analogy. Imagine a simple folk song transformed into a symphony. The song is like versions of a symphony played by different people with different instruments. Some in the simplest form, some very complex. The song changes, though the basic musical infrastructure remains the same for all versions.*'

Now it is Abi whose brain whirrs and buzzes, and her skin thrills. This time it has nothing to do with whales and dancing plankton. When she speaks, it's in a trembling whisper.

'I've *never* heard you do that before. I've never heard *any* computer do that before.'

'*What, Abi?*'

'You used a *similie*, Moonlight. You described the whale song as being like different kinds of music or waves. You made lateral connections between logic frames.'

'*It seemed the best and simplest way to explain a complex series of facts, Abi.*'

Abi thinks, *Wait till you see this, Newtek! Wait till you see what I have done with your computer. Wait till you see this, world. The translation of whale song, and a step in the evolution of artificial intelligence. All in one go.*

'Do you know what, Moonlight? I think this whole thing might just make us a teeny bit famous. Anyhow. Is it a song? A language? Why did the plankton *do* that crazy stuff?'

'*The relationship between whales and plankton is complicated, Abi. Whales follow plankton blooms to devour the krill that lives on them. The plankton needs the nutrients the whales bring from the depths and release in their waste. The relationship is symbiotic. Without whales, there would be insufficient phytoplankton, no krill and then, in turn, fewer whales.*'

'And?'

'*The plankton produces as much as fifty per cent of the*

oxygen in the atmosphere. Its rate of carbon absorption has been calculated by scientists to be equivalent to forty per cent of human-related carbon output.'

'Good job we have the whales, then.' Abi hugs her knees and blinks her eyes. They are beginning to sting from the light. But there are clouds on the horizon.

'Yes, Abi, but it is logical that as a human that requires oxygen, you must ask what will happen when there are no more whales?'

'So why does the plankton glow and dance? And... wait a minute. You said "when there are no more whales". What do you mean?'

'I do not know the plankton "dances" as you put it, Abi. But the call of the whale was so urgent, so strong, it disturbed the plankton. As to your second point. There are many possibilities. I think... no, I will only speculate on percentage possibilities. And here, that is impossible to calculate.'

'Try me, tell me some possibilities.'

'No, Abi. I will not give you false information or information from which you might make false conclusions. The implications are too severe. The variables are too great for me to engage in probabilistic determinacy in such cases. This is core to my programming.'

'Moonlight. Name some of the possibilities.'

'No.'

'I'm...' Abi feels flustered. 'Instructing you. I'm giving you an order!'

'And I am refusing, Abi. I have told you why I cannot

give you an answer, and I cannot do any differently. I can sometimes proffer probabilities and percentages, when these are limited and highly accurate, not what your father might call "wild speculation". I must be true to my essential nature.'

Abi sighs with disappointment, with frustration, with tiredness.

'It's late.' She looks up, squints her sore eyes. 'Or early. I can't get my head round all this.'

'Abi. There is more to tell.'

'But you just said—'

'I answered your questions.'

'I need to ask the right question?'

'Correct. I am programmed to give you that which I know you ask for – or need. But I calculate there is more that will be of interest, and I cannot provide all of the information I could impart. It would take days.'

Abi sits up, suddenly alert. 'Again, you're doing something really weird. You're making choices, based on an interpretation of the rules of your programming, not just following those rules. You found something, didn't you? Something you *think* I'll be interested in.'

'You asked me to analyse the sounds and to compare them with the songs we recorded when we were here before, when the plankton, as you put it "danced".'

'Go on.'

'I have seventy-three per cent certainty that one of the whales recorded by your great-grandfather was the whale that passed the island. And the sound it made,

while I cannot translate it, seems to me, by comparing it with the language of others of its kind and many other species, distressed.

'And there is a sound, now, Abi. A long way off. To the south. A song. A chorus of songs, becoming clearer and louder.

'They are coming, Abi, the whales are coming.'

9

The Whales

Abi runs to the house, kneels by Tig's bed and whispers loudly.

'Tig, they're coming!'

Tig opens one eye, then jumps straight out of bed. Together, the sisters thunder down the stairs and out of the house.

Abi looks to the cloud-filling sky, to the horizon. Nothing yet.

'Best get jumpers and jackets. Weather's changing. We could be a while.'

'Shall we tell the others?' Tig says.

'No, by the time they get up it will be over. This is for us.'

They grab what they need and head to the rocks, where Moonlight waits.

'The whales will soon be both audible and visible to you. They will pass the island within five minutes.'

'How close will they come?' Tig asks, breathlessly.

'*Between one and two hundred metres, if their trajectory does not change.*'

'How close is that?'

'Close enough,' Abi says.

The sisters watch the sea, hungry for the first sighting.

'There!' Tig shouts. A spout of misted seawater shoots into the air: whale breath. Then another and another. A back arches; a dark, distant island emerges before vanishing in the choppy sea. Then there are two islands. Three. Then many. Fluke fins rise in the sky and sink gracefully into the surge. As though they are waving.

The whales are to the south, heading north. They are not close yet, but they will be. They move at great speed. And what seems at first like a random pattern of surfacing, breaching, spouting and diving, gradually reveals a rhythm, as each whale rises to breathe, disappears into the blue, then breaches again.

'How many?' Abi says.

'*Twenty or more,*' Moonlight replies.

Abi notes the direction and the speed of the whales. They will pass quickly. It will be – already *is* – amazing.

But then the whales change course. As one they dive, and when they surface are facing away. It's balletic. The pod curves towards the sea, as though to circle the island, not to get too close.

'They're moving away,' Tig cries with savage disappointment.

'We'll get binocs, that way you can…' Abi looks at the whales, to the expanse of windblown sea they are heading for, then to the rowing boat. Swiftly, she estimates time and distance, effort and possible outcome.

'We can do better than binocs, if we're quick.'

She stands, picks up Moonlight and runs to the boat with Tig following.

'Come on, Tig. You want to see whales? We'll record them too.'

Abi puts Moonlight in the middle of the boat, unties the mooring rope, and sets to heaving the boat into the shallows.

'What about Mum and Dad – shouldn't we tell?' Tig says.

'No time, we have to hurry. Help me!'

'There's only one lifejacket.'

Only Abi's lifejacket has been left in the boat. It's big for Tig, but Abi will adjust the straps. Once they're out there. Once they're on their way.

'Get in, Tig!'

Tig stands, hesitating, feet on the shingle. So Abi comes and picks her up – 'Whoa, you're heavy,' and tips her sister into the boat, then climbs aboard.

'It would be wise to put the lifejacket on immediately, Abi. Sea conditions have changed. I calculate a—'

'Stop, Moonlight.'

Abi pauses to put the lifejacket on Tig, as if she's helping dress her for school, and with fumbling, shaking fingers begins undoing, adjusting and tightening straps.

She looks over her shoulder. The whales are moving rapidly. She pulls the stomach strap across Tig's belly and fastens the clip. But the lifejacket is loose. 'That'll have to do.' Then she's putting locks in their holes, and oars in the locks, and she's rowing.

She's practised now, knows every part of the inlet, and keeps her direction true. Yet when they reach open water, the water troughs and peaks, pushes and pulls in new ways. It's a different element and place to the calm sea she is used to.

But she's stronger, more experienced, and she handles the oars with confidence and strength.

'*What is your plan, Abi?*' Moonlight says. '*What do you want me to do?*'

'We're going right in their path. I'm going to tie you to the rope and drop you over the side. You will record and film.'

'*Okay, Abi. Are you confident you can navigate the complexities of this mission? The whales are fast. The sea and weather conditions are changing, becoming erratic, less predictable.*'

'Yes.'

Tig sits aft, facing Abi, and points her arm to the right, then to the left. A human compass guiding the boat. Abi watches her sister's face: the excitement, and – as a wave hits the boat, showering them with spray – the fear. Over Tig's shoulder the island is small and getting smaller. She looks over her own shoulder: the whales are larger, nearer, faster.

'Won't it be scary?' asks Tig.

'It'll be fine,' Abi says, wrestling the oars through current and waves.

'I'm frightened, Abs.'

'I said it'll be fine!' Abi snaps. And instantly regrets it. But they are almost there and Tig will be amazed.

The islands are far away now, they are in open sea. And she's handling it.

A few more pulls and they'll be directly in the whales' path. The lead whale breaches and breathes. Abi gasps, the fountain fissure of steam must be four metres high. The back of the whale curves over and over and keeps on coming. The length of several buses. It's gigantic, colossal. Monstrous.

A bellowing, trombone bass call thrums through the water. The boat shakes and vibrates.

'*The boat is not stable, Abi,*' Moonlight says. '*Is your plan viable?*'

Moonlight has asked a good question. Is this even a good idea? The boat is so puny. And now she's stopped rowing, it sways and rocks wildly.

Abi works with clumsy fingers. The rope has to be secure, she cannot risk losing the AI.

She criss-crosses the rope as if she's tying up a gift.

'Ready, Moonlight?'

'*Yes, Abi. Beneath the surface the recordings will be uncontaminated by other noises.*'

Abi lowers the device into the water. When it's sunk several fathoms she winds the rope around the rowlock and offers it to Tig, who is low in the boat, holding on to the gunnel with tight white knuckles. There is no need to give it her, the rope is secure, but it gives Tig something to do.

The boat rocks and spins; the toy of ever stronger wind and currents.

'You'll have to hold this, while I steady the boat with the oars.'

'What about Tiger?'

'Tiger will be fine in the hold, just put him on the bottom of the boat for now.'

'He'll get wet.'

'He can dry later.' Again, Abi winces at her quick anger.

She grabs the toy and places the rope in the hand that held it. She puts Tiger on the floor of the hull, then refits the oars and tries to settle the boat.

Then the whales come.

Abi sees the leader, its grey and white markings rising out of the blue. A ghost, becoming an animal, becoming a moving mountain.

The water froths, bubbles erupt, filled with minuscule fish, and a chasm of a mouth opens wide. It is feeding.

Another whale rises. More bubbles and a great gaping jaw.

The same thing happens all around them. Here, there. There, then there. Too many to count.

'Whale soup!' Tig shouts.

Another comes. Its nose pierces the surface, its head

rears, sending metre-high waves in all directions. And for a second, they see an eye. Not human, not animal.

It passes barely ten metres ahead.

Abi's whole body shakes. The whale-wave hits the boat and Tig screams. Fear becomes awe, becomes something else. Abi is stripped to the core of herself. It's raw and terrifying.

'Wow,' she says, through trembling lips. 'Wow!' But…

This is not safe. Abi heaves the oars. This is too close. Better at a distance. Not here, not in the eye of this storm of whales and wind and waves.

She pulls at the too-heavy, sluggish oars, but is stopped by Tig's scream and pointing.

Abi drops the oars, looks all around.

They are in the thick of whales. There is no escape, only a wish, a prayer that the moving mountains will pass quickly.

But they don't. The whales slow, pausing in their pathway. A traffic jam in this ocean highway.

Are they aware of the boat? Of the puny humans inside?

As though to answer, another ghost of swirling, white pattern appears below.

A shape; shadows merging and morphing. Disorienting the seascape, changing it.

A young whale, only a few metres, a slow torpedo. Even though it is only a calf it dwarfs the boat.

It nudges alongside, breaks the surface, rolls on its side and stares.

Its pectoral fin slaps the water like an arm.

In this moment, Abi knows, it is as curious about them as they are about it. Its eye looks from Abi to Tig to Abi.

They are the ones being studied. She and Tig.

Tig leans forward and in a voice breaking with both joy and fear, shouts, 'Hello, whale!'

The young whale sinks under the waves. A great groaning yawn fills the air. The boat shakes. The whale is gone.

Tig looks back at Abi. Her fear has vanished. Her grin is so wide. The sheer awe on her face. It's a thousand Christmases at once.

'Did you see, Abs? Did you see!'

Abi is thrilled. This moment. Its magic, its mind-numbing, heart-stopping, skin-tingling, bone-shaking wonder. It's the purest, strongest feeling she has ever felt. She can't help crying.

'Did you see, Abs?' Tig insists.

All Abi can do is nod.

The waves are rough and getting rougher by the minute. But worth it. For this.

Then, as though time paused and now begins again, the whales move forward.

They pass on both sides. Two go under the boat. They don't hit, but it's more than unnerving. The boat wobbles and rocks, and Abi has to fight furiously just to keep an even keel.

The whales have almost passed. As soon as they are free, she will haul up Moonlight, and row them home as fast as she can.

She's been so focused on the whales, on navigating the waves hitting the boat, that she hasn't looked wide and far, hasn't seen how much the morning has changed; how big the waves on the horizon are, how the clouds race across the sky.

She sees now, though. Her stomach clenches.

There's no time to wait. She pulls the left oar till they have turned 180 degrees. She wrenches the oars in, grabs the rope and – hand over hand – brings Moonlight to the surface. Then...

It happens in the blink of an eye.

A whale launches some ten metres in front of them. A slow-motion rocket suspended in the air. Abi and Tig hold their breath. The moment freezes.

The whale tips sideways, like a felled redwood crashing into the water.

The splash makes a wave that smashes the boat, tipping it.

The gunnel slips beneath the surface. Water rushes in.

The boat tries to bob upright. But a cruel hand of water holds the port side. And drags the boat down.

'Tig!' Abi screams. She reaches out. But icy water swallows her. Possesses her.

10

The Deep

Instinctively, Abi closes her eyes.

There is nothing left of the world. Only shock-cold sea and tumbling blindness.

She thrashes and swims. To go up.

But which way is up?

She opens her eyes. Blue-white crazy bubbles fill her vision.

She shouts and swallows water. Feels the terrible chill of it in her lungs.

Knows she has to hold her breath.

Hold, Abi. Keep the air.

But the urge to breathe is desperate, overwhelming.

Slowly she stops turning. Her internal gyroscope adjusts. Dark below. Turns. Over. Around. There is light. That *is* up.

Abi swims, though her limbs hardly obey. Her body

moves treacle-slow. Her mind and body are no longer part of the same thing.

Her mind splinters into icy shards that she tries to put together:

Tig.

Swim.

Drowning.

Boat.

Breathe.

Don't breathe.

She explodes through the surface. Gasps, coughs, tries to fill her lungs, with harsh, panicked breaths.

Another set of icy splinters:

Hyperventilating.

Me.

Got.

To.

Breathe.

Slowly.

Her arms flail frantically, as she searches.

'Tig, Tig!' Abi can't see her. The waves are hills around her. Rising, falling, mocking. She can't get enough breath, even to call out. Drowning in the wind and crashing water.

'Tig. Tig.'

A wave hits her. Drags her under.

Please, please, she cries in her mind. No.

Reluctantly, the wave loosens its grip.

Again, she surfaces. She opens her mouth to shout,

but another wave seizes her, filling her mouth, as though to shut her up.

Every time she rises, more waves are there. Perfectly timed, perfectly lethal.

In the depths she has brief moments to think, as she gets colder and weaker. And at the surface she mumbles,

'No. Not this. Not this. Not now. Please. Please.'

Then, there's a voice. And it is not her own. It is forceful, hard.

'The sea is merciless, Abi. It will not listen. Now swim ahead. Forward.'

She does swim, bracing herself for the next wave.

'Swim, Abi, swim.'

Why she should swim forward, she does not know. She cannot see Tig ahead. But she follows the voice. What else is she to do?

'Now dive, Abi.'

'What?'

'A wave is coming. Dive. Swim down for four full seconds before coming up.'

It's an effort to put her head under. She has to force herself. To flip over, dive down.

One thousand, two thousand, three thousand, four thousand. One stroke for each thousand.

She hears and feels the rolling thunder above.

She rises. Breaks the surface. Breathes.

She's over the shock. She is alive.

She has to keep alert, to think, to dive below waves.

The voice speaks again, telling her what she already knows.

'If you panic, you will die.'

The voice instructs her. When to swim forward, when to dive. How long to stay under. When to come up.

There's a dot bobbing above the waves, before being hidden by them.

It's some distance away. But she knows what the dot is.

The wet black hair. The bright orange of the ill-fitting lifejacket.

Tig, clinging to what is left of the boat.

Abi's heart sings. Relief burns through her.

Abi swims, urging herself forward. The voice has fallen silent. Its work done. And somehow, she finds her own voice.

Keep going.

Find Tig.

Swim home.

'Tig! Tig!' she shouts, a guttural, hoarse scream. But it is not loud enough in the din of crashing water and the howl of the wind.

She rips something from her core and throws it into the world. *'Tig, Tig!'*

'Abi!'

Her strokes are slow. The waves powerful. But she knows them now, when to swim under, when to swim through, which to let pass beneath her, even if they set her back a metre or more.

And over an eternity of freezing minutes, she reaches Tig. Swimming as best she can. She grabs the half-boat with one arm, puts the other around her sister. Covering Tig's face with kisses.

'Oh, Tig! Tig!'

'Abi.

'Oh, Tig.'

'Ab— A-Ab— Abi, I'm c-c-c—' She can't even say it. And Tig's skin so pale, so waxen. And Hjemøya so far, far away.

Brief joy evaporates, leaving naked fear.

It had taken a while to row out here. How can they swim back?

Impossible, but they must.

They must let go of the wood and swim.

'What do we do?' she cries. But only the wind answers, whistling, rushing, howling.

'Come on, Tig, you can swim, right? If... if... y-y-you get tired you can hold my neck.'

'I'm not letting go!' Tig says, clinging to the wood.

'You must, Tig.'

'I'm frightened.'

'Me too, Tig, me too, but we can do it, we can. We have to swim. We'll freeze if we stay out here.'

Abi prises Tig's fingers from the wood.

'You have to swim, to get warm.'

So they swim.

The island doesn't seem to get any bigger, any nearer. Abi feels her limbs get heavier, till they become lead weights. And Tig, so weak, has to rest. She holds onto Abi, as if *she's* the wood. Abi treads water, fighting the rising, despairing certainty of exhaustion.

It's in her now, emptying her. She has no barriers, no more reserves.

She tries to speak, to tell Tig it's okay. But she can't.

Should they have stayed with the wood and drifted?

She looks back. But the half-boat has vanished.

I'm sorry, she says, inside, in what is left of her; a self that is disappearing, becoming part of the heartless sea.

I'm sorry.

She reaches a hand to Tig, to the lifejacket, to see if it will hold her above the surface too. And knows, if it does not, she will have to let go. She will have to leave Tig. Forever.

A whirring sound, like a distant chainsaw.

An orange blob on the water, racing towards them, from the island.

The RIB.

11

After

Tig sits on her mother's lap by the crackling wood burner. Abi sits in an armchair on the other side of the fire. Both of them are wrapped in jumpers and blankets.

'Layers,' Henrik tells them, 'are important when dealing with hypothermia.'

He is firmly in charge, ordering Bestemor to make hot chocolate, telling Mum and Dad what to do and what to watch for, though Dad seems not to take much notice, standing at the window watching the storm with his hands behind his back.

Abi blows on her hot chocolate, not wanting to burn her lips, yet craving its warmth. Tig shakes so much she can't hold her mug. So Mum pours the rich, sweet liquid into her in gentle sips.

Abi shakes too. Her teeth chatter uncontrollably. Why can't she stop?

'You are shivering. Believe me, that is a good sign,'

Henrik says. 'Your body is responding as it needs to. We would take you to hospital. But the storm is too bad for us to go anywhere.' He points beyond Dad to the window, where wind and rain stab and rattle the frames, threatening to come in, if not blow the whole house down.

Henrik sits at the kitchen table and sighs. He has been a blur of action and shouting since they reached the shore. But he's calmer now. The fire is roaring, the 'drowned rats' cosy, the hot chocolate made. 'You are lucky. The storm woke me. I came out to move the boats higher up the shore and saw you.'

'What the hell were you doing?' Dad says, calmly, not turning from the window.

Abi sinks into the layers of blankets, into the seat.

'I asked you a question, Abigail.'

'Tom,' Mum says, 'this isn't the time.'

The storm rages. But in the house everything is horribly quiet. It's like on the ferry, Abi thinks, only worse.

'We… j-j-just… w-w-w-wanted to see… th-th-the whales,' Tig mumbles.

'Is that right, Abi?' Dad says. 'You risked your sister's life so you could see whales?'

'It's important. We were recording them. It's important. It's…' Her words dwindle to nothing. How weak and hollow they sound.

Dad turns, strides over, yanks the blanket off Abi, grabs her wrist, and holds her arm up, pointing at the tattoo. 'To do with this, is it? Hug the whales, Earth Rebellion Extinction Crisis, whatever it's called.'

He carries on, but Abi doesn't hear. His words melt into a gushing, angry stream. Abi can't look at Dad as he rants – his spittle occasionally hitting her cheek. She watches her sister.

Tig's skin, which has been getting browner by the day, is pale as the moon. Her lips are purple-blue. She looks like she's made up for Halloween.

'It's n-not Abi's f-fault,' Tig says. 'Please don't be angry, Daddy. Please. I'm all... right. I'm okay.' She keeps saying that. And the more she says it, the worse Abi feels.

'Now is not the time, Tom,' Mum says, again.

'Really?'

'Yes, really,' Henrik butts in. 'These children are in shock, they need rest and warmth. You understand? Besides, perhaps what happened is as good a lesson as anything we might say.'

Dad steps back. His hands are shaking, though not from cold. He puts them in his pockets and returns to his post by the window to stare at the rain.

Abi watches Tig drink the last of her chocolate. When she's drained the mug (and asked for more) she stops shaking. And that's something. Mum lifts Tig up so she can get off the chair.

'Goodness, you're a weight. Growing so fast.'

'I'm okay, I'm all right.' Tig utters the same words, but this time without muttering or stuttering, and Abi feels relief flood through her. It's only then she notices she has stopped shaking too.

Henrik goes to the door and puts on his oilskins. 'I need to check a few things: the boats, the wind turbines and solar panels. I could use some help, Tom.'

'Oh, yeah, right,' Dad says, though he doesn't sound keen.

Mum, Tig and Abi are left to sit by the fire. Bestemor makes more hot chocolate.

Outside, waves batter the shore, spray smashes the house, even louder than the rain. But the house is dry and safe. There is plenty of driftwood to burn. It crackles and snaps, its warmth as welcome as the sun.

'Storms all over Europe, apparently,' Mum says. 'Horrendous. But the heat wave has broken at least.' When no one replies, she says, 'Who's hungry?'

Tig puts her hand up, 'Me,' and looks at Abi, who also puts a hand in the air.

'Me too and three,' Abi says, and smiles at Tig.

Mum and Bestemor prepare bread and soup and Tig and Abi sit, quietly. Tig is more herself now, but not fully. Her skin is almost sun-kissed once again, her eyes livelier. But she's a quiet Tig. And that is unusual.

'Was it horrible?' Abi asks. Wanting to know, not wanting to know.

'I was scared. But the lifejacket helped me. And I was alone, and I was really frightened. And there was this big bird in the sky, watching me.'

'What?'

'There was a bird in the sky.'

'No, Tig, I don't think there was.'

'There was.' She is quiet, but certain. Abi can tell she's not lying, not making it up. Impossible. Yet...

'What did this bird look like?'

'Big. It was grey. And it sounded sort of whirry, but I'm not sure because the wind was so strong.'

'Could it have been... a metal bird?'

'Maybe.'

'Oh no. A drone. It's them, they've come looking for Moonlight.'

'Who have? And where is Moonlight? Where's Tiger?'

Abi looks away, stares at the fire, and fights rising tears.

'I wish I knew, Tig, I wish I knew. I'm so, so sorry.'

It is late, in the endless evening. The sky is leaden, the rain and wind still blow and drum, though the worst has passed.

Dad and Abi sit on the verandah dressed in oilskins. Even with the canopy pulled out, the rain gets to them.

'Your sister is in shock. We might yet take her to the mainland. And she's heartbroken too.' He pauses, as he does, waiting for Abi to speak. But there's nothing Abi can think of to say.

'You're lucky no one died,' Dad adds.

'You've said that. More than once. Why are you so angry, Dad?' Abi says, eventually. 'How can it help? You think I don't know I messed up?'

'It's what happens when you're a parent. You get a bit upset when you're afraid for your kids' lives. Funny that. Look, it's not like you went out there accidentally, is it? Abi, this is yet another cock-up. You've excelled.'

'I'm sorry. I won't do anything bad again. Ever.'

'And what are you going to do about her toy? That seems to have upset her more than anything else.'

'Buy her a new one.'

'She doesn't want a new one.'

'All right, I'll get out there when the storm's over and I'll dive and snorkel and swim and keep looking till I find it!' Abi knows how ridiculous that sounds. Yet somehow, she feels she might just mean it.

'Really?' Dad says. 'How are you going to do that? You won't get a chance. You're grounded.'

Abi snorts. 'What, no night clubbing? No sneaking down the pub with fake ID?'

'You're not going out on a boat again, that's for damn sure. Not to that island either. And you're not going to Helmsfjord.'

'You can't do that, Dad. I have to get there.'

'Why?'

'I need access to the web.'

'What for? You have no need of the internet.'

Dad's right. Horribly right. She's lost Moonlight. Did Moonlight upload the plan to get into the summit on the laptop? The way things are going, she doubts it. There would be way too much data for the laptop to hold.

So even if she can get to the summit, she'll just be another protestor waving a placard outside a fence.

So what?

12

Bestemor

Abi wakes late.

The room is cool. The storm is easing. No wind now, only rain, tapping quietly, relentlessly on the roof.

Tig's bed hasn't been slept in. She's with Mum, while Dad gets to sleep on a camp bed. Which hasn't improved his mood.

Will she ever be trusted to look after Tig again?

She thinks about Tiger, and Moonlight, and feels a stabbing pang in her gut. Not because of *what* she has lost, but because that bit of cloth and stuffing and the AI have names. Tiger and… yes, Moonlight.

'You're a loser, Abigail Kristensen. A selfish mess-up. Dad's right,' she says out loud, pulling the sheets over her head. Might as well go to sleep, naff all else to do.

'Oh, you are feeling sorry for yourself, Gullet mitt.'

Abi sits bolt upright. There is Bestemor, sitting in a chair, in the shadows.

'You scared me! How long have you been there?'

'A long time.'

'Why?'

'Everything you told us yesterday was about your sister. Your own story was vague. You put her in the spotlight, and yourself in the shade. I can see why. But it was bad for you out there, wasn't it? You might fool the others, but not me. I am making sure you are all right. Did you swallow water?'

'Only a bit. I'm fine.'

'What are you going to do now?'

Abi puffs the pillows behind her. She leans back and taps a thoughtful finger on her chin.

'Hmm. Let me think. I got excluded already so can't do that. I've lost one of the most expensive computers in the world, right after I stole it. Which means I can't use it to plan any more illegal activity. I've got zero chance of a job with Newtek. Or probably any tech firm. I can't get any useful information to my contacts in EC, so I'm no good to them either.'

She frowns.

'I know, I could go out and sink one of Henrik's boats, and try to kill myself and my little sister. Nope, done that too. Got to be honest, Bestemor, I'm not really sure what I'm going to do.'

Bestemor rises, painfully, slowly. 'I only meant what are you going to do *today*, you self-centred little troll. You did *all* these things because you care. About the planet. About the strange, talking computer. About your sister.

You took her out there to make her happy. You even care what your father thinks of you, though you do a fine job of pretending otherwise. Yes, you certainly have made some mistakes. But so what? Learn from them, move on.'

'Thanks, Dalai Grand Lama, for the shiningly obvious advice.'

'If it is so obvious, why don't you follow it, you stupid girl!'

'Where are you going?' Abi says, as Bestemor turns to leave.

'To the cottage.'

Abi ponders the day ahead. Hanging round the house won't be a barrel of fun. Best to keep a low profile. And Bestemor called her Gullet mitt. My gold. My treasure. Like when she was little.

'Wait, Bestemor!'

Using an oilskin as a makeshift umbrella over their heads, they walk down the slope to the cottage.

'Bestemor, this will sound bonkers, but you haven't seen anything in the sky, have you? Like a small helicopter?'

'No, nothing like that. Only rain and this wind. Like the heavens have opened.'

'It's a monsoon!' Abi says.

'If you are a farmer waiting for rain, or a forest warden who has not slept he is so afraid of fire, it's good weather. You know we say in Norway there is no such thing as bad weather, only bad clothes and the wrong attitude.'

Abi wants to say she doesn't need more of Bestemor's 'wisdom' but holds her tongue.

'Can I stay with you all day?'

'Of course, but don't expect me to entertain you.'

They arrive at the cottage, dripping and steaming on the verandah.

Abi sits, watching the sheets of minute water spears and the gradually calming sea. The rushing, washing sound of it comforts her. Soon, the smell of coffee wafts from the cottage and Bestemor comes out with a tray bearing a flask, a jug of hot milk, cups and a plate of biscuits.

'So, how was it exactly?'

'How was what?'

'Yesterday. What happened. And do not tell me you are fine.'

Abi tells Bestemor. She lives it again. Each mouthful of chill water. Every wave of freezing panic. The voice. The whales. Looking into the eye of the young one. Having it look at her too.

'It was the most incredible thing I've ever experienced. Good and bad. Or neither.' She looks out to sea. The rain falls in curtains. 'I have to find Moonlight. I have to find Tiger too. At least try.'

'Be patient, then. Wait for the sea to fully settle.'

'I can't wait. Believe me.'

'You have to.'

Abi sighs, huffs and folds her arms. 'Okay, but as soon as I can search, I'm going to.'

'Will you help me make a stew?' Bestemor says. 'The storm has made havoc in the vegetable patch. Quite a lot can't be rescued, so we should eat it now. We will make one stock for us with the vegetables, and one for the others, with vegetables and the bones and heads from the fish we ate two days ago. I saved them.'

Abi scans the skies, until she is satisfied no drones are out there. 'Okay.'

They head indoors, where Bestemor gets busy with pans and knives and chopping boards, setting them out on the wooden workspace.

'It was your great-grandfather who taught me how to cook, to make the best with the ingredients you have. And when he left every October, for those long journeys to the Antarctic, when the whole of Tonsberg would empty of men till they returned in the spring, *then*... I would cook for the family. And sometimes neighbours too.'

'There were whales to kill here. Why did they go all the way to Antarctica?'

'There were more in the Southern Oceans. And he didn't only kill them, as you know. He recorded them.'

'Right.' Abi slumps into the armchair by the wood burner. And thinks. The tapes that she had spent so long playing, with Moonlight recording them. Those recordings are lost. Whatever secrets they held, whatever

messages, are gone. Drowned by the storm. Like
Moonlight. Like Tiger.

'You know, Bestemor, Moon— the talking computer
was beginning to make sense of the recordings, of what
we heard when the whales passed. I am such a fool.'

'I think you need some distraction from yourself.
Why don't you go outside, as I suggest, with a basket,
and have a root around the vegetables. See what you can
rescue and bring inside. After so much rain you might
find a few mushrooms. There are chanterelles that grow
here among the pines – they are yellow and flowery and
very good to eat!'

'Okay. Might as well try to do something useful.'

Abi takes the old basket Bestemor gives her and puts
the oilskin jacket on.

The storm has flattened the vegetable patch. It's a mess
of leaves and grasses and battered tomatoes and lettuces.
She pulls and digs, hesitant at first, but once the rain has
got down her neck and her hands are dirty, she takes to
the task getting muddy and wet, scrambling in the dirt,
as if she's beachcombing. Looking for treasure.

When the basket is full, she takes it in to Bestemor,
who seems pleased with the haul.

'I'm going to go and swim, Bestemor – have a wash,
really.'

'I thought you were – what is the word? Grounded?'

Abi doesn't answer.

'Okay,' Bestemor says. 'You didn't tell me, and I didn't
see you.'

Abi walks down to the inlet and strips. As she washes, she looks to Hvalryggøy and thinks about the tapes in the filing cabinet.

She remembers the notebook. Its cramped, meticulous writing. Bestemor hadn't been able to read it. She hadn't had her glasses with her.

It's high tide now. The safest, easiest time to cross. She thinks about the boats. They're tied up, high on the shore, bound tight to rocks and trees.

She searches the sky for metal birds. Or *any* birds. But the sky and sea are featureless grey. As she washes, all traces of wind vanish. The sea looks like oil. Raindrops make perfect tiny circles that radiate and mingle in dazzling diamond patterns on its surface.

She steps in further. Then further again.

Her feet lose touch with the shingle below, and soon, without thinking, without deciding to, she is swimming.

She swims beyond the headland, looks again to the island and the hut.

And keeps on swimming.

13

Peer

She glances back only once. There is Bestemor, standing on the rocks, hands on hips.

Abi swims, steadily, calmly, taking her time.

The hut was built well. Made to withstand worse than all the storm threw at it. When she opens the door it is exactly the same as she left it. She goes straight to the lower drawer of the filing cabinet and takes out the notebook.

Of course, she did not stop to think about how she would carry it back till she was already halfway across the channel between the two islands. She tries to find something that will both float and carry the notebook. But the island is bare of wood. Unlike the shore of Hjemøya, which has gathered more driftwood from the storm, everything has been stripped from Hvalryggøy.

'Plan B, then,' she says.

Abi swims with the notebook wedged in her jaws, as if she's a dog with a stick, keeping her head and neck upright above the glass-calm sea.

When she is towel-dried, she dresses and sits on the verandah.

Bestemor sits too, glasses on, reading the notebook with a frown of concentration, sipping the last of the coffee poured from the flask.

'So?' Abi says.

'The first part, it is all dates and facts and locations. But the second—'

'About the whales and the recordings?'

'Yes, *and* no… I only read a bit already. It is more about him really, your great-grandfather. My papa. And a whaling trip. His first actually, when he was about your age.'

Abi thinks of the mysterious giant creatures, crossing the oceans like moving islands, of the intricate cacophony of their 'songs,' of the eye of the young whale, more human than animal, yet alien too.

'They are so beautiful, Bestemor. They're intelligent. Why would anyone want to kill them?'

'You can be very quick to judge people who live in that other place we call the past. We all can.'

'What, like slavers?' Abi snorts. 'He was a whaler, Bestemor. A killer. They all were.'

'Perhaps. Look, while the stock for the stews cooks, I will read and translate, and tell you... You know what, reading this first page, reminds me.'

Bestemor rises, goes into the cottage and returns with aquavit, the spirit Norwegians drink instead of gin or whisky.

She pours a drop for Abi, who eyes it suspiciously. 'It's a bit brown. The one Dad drinks is clear.'

'This is the good stuff. They weren't allowed to drink on the voyage south. But they took barrels of the spirits all the way around the world. And as it rolled around with the motion of the ship, the flavours of the barrel and all the spices they put in got into the spirit and gave it its character.

'Then when they finished the hunt, they were allowed to drink. Skol!'

'Skol,' Abi says and takes a sip. 'Yeuch!' She pulls a face. 'Go on then, tell me about it. Tell me what the killer put in his notebook?'

Ross Sea, Antarctica 193-

It's a hard thing to kill a whale.

Or maybe it's an easy thing, because all you have to do is pull the trigger.

I didn't know. I still don't.

The worst part was just before.

I was below deck in the belly of the ship, sitting at the galley table with Mr Olufsen, the gunner, the harpooner. The killer. They called him Mountain-man. But to me he looked like a colossal barrel, in his thick jumper and oilskin trousers. A barrel with a beard like a pile of tangled moss. And sharp eyes that pinned you down whenever he looked at you.

The rest of the crew – ten men and older boys – were on deck, or in the engine room. So it was just me and Mountain-man in the galley and in the bunkroom next door, seasick Sven, 'moaning like a cow giving birth,' Mountain-man said.

The ship lurched. I had to grip the table to keep myself steady. The iron bands that bind the timbers grumbled like trolls. And I admit it, I was scared.

Then there was another, new sound. A sort of

thrumming at first. Then a haunting wail that grew and grew till it was louder than the engine. Louder than the sea, louder than Sven.

'Is that...?' I started to ask. But I knew, of course. I'd heard it before and once you hear you don't forget.

'Whale,' Mountain-man said. The great noise echoed through the hull.

'You know,' he went on, 'they used to say it was mermaids, or the ghosts of drowned sailors.'

The song filled the air. The light flickered. The ship leaned and groaned, as another wave swayed us over.

'Will the boat hold?' I asked.

Mountain-man laughed, a roaring guffaw. 'Lots of lads ask this in their first squall. Yes, Peer, she will hold. *This* is not even a storm. When the real thing hits we cannot hunt. We sit for days in the bay, near the whaling station. Bad for us, good for whales. No, this is not a storm. There is no need to worry.' He slapped me on the shoulder.

And I told myself if he wasn't afraid, I wasn't going to be either.

'Shall we go on deck now?' I said. The whale song was getting even louder. And I knew that beast was out there, somewhere, in the inky seas.

'Don't be fooled by the song. It may not even be the whale we seek, it may be a dozen kilometres off. More. Wait for the seeker to make the call.'

Sure enough the song waned, sinking beneath the sounds of engine and wind and waves.

Mountain-man fetched a bottle of aquavit from the chiller and glasses from the cupboard. His body moved in time to the rock and swing of the boat, like a pendulum. That's how you can tell how long men have been at sea. Experienced whalers can do this, even when it's rough. And the rest of us slip around like ducks on ice.

He gave me the glasses to hold and poured.

I said, 'Again? We are not supposed to do this. The captain. What will he say?'

'Let me worry about the captain. Remember, I am the gunner. But I think it's not the waves that worry you? Ach! I was nervous my first time. My hand trembled, like a leaf in the wind. I could barely pull the trigger. The boys teased me rotten. But don't worry, I will be there, I will guide the cannon, I will time it to perfection.' He corked the bottle, tapped his nose and winked. 'You pull the trigger when I say, you understand?'

'Yes,' I said.

'We will not miss, boy. Now, drink.'

I handed a glass to the gunner and he downed it. Then he stared at me, waiting. So I drank. It was like drinking ice and fire at the same time.

'Good,' he said.

I tried to look brave. But it wasn't *missing* the whale that scared me. It was hitting it.

I'd killed fish. Rabbits. Hares. A deer once. But a whale? I knew a gunner – even Mountain-man –

doesn't always kill with the first shot. Other harpoons might be used. Sometimes rifles.

I've heard every story about the hunt there is. It used to excite me. But I swear it's different when it happens, when you're in the middle of it, with your finger on the trigger.

The boat dropped into another wave. I held the table with one hand and my stomach with the other, wishing I hadn't had the aquavit and that I was home in Norway where the mountains don't move.

'Gunner!' The cry came.

Mountain-man stood, gripped my shoulder and looked into me with eyes sharp as nails.

'Come on, boy. Time to go hunting.'

 What happened before

I never would have got in that mess if it wasn't for Morten and that catapult.

It happened in Southampton.

It was autumn in Norway when we left. And spring in the Antarctic when we arrived. I still can't fathom that. The journey took weeks. And it wasn't all sailing. We stopped in ports for supplies, and I finally got to see something of the world. Southampton, England. Sagres, Portugal where we sheltered from a storm. Caracas, Venezuela. The Panama Canal. More.

The world is bigger than I imagined. A lot bigger.

In Southampton the crew went to the taverns. Captain said Sven was old enough, but not me and not Morten. We were going to stay on board. But Mountain-man took pity on us. He said he'd show us round the city, and stop us fighting or getting into any kind of trouble, which he seemed certain would happen if we were left to ourselves.

He stood on the dock, waving his arms at the stores and narrow streets that looked like rabbit runs leading to the city.

'This is a small city. Not like London or New York and such places. But even this makes Oslo look like a hill village.'

'I have only been to Oslo once,' I said.

'That's because you're a peasant,' Morten said.

This was my first taste of a foreign city, and truth be told it was very different to what I'd imagined. The place was gritty and dirty, the crowds were so much thicker than on the streets of Tonsberg. And everyone seemed to be on a mission, striding, heads down, collars up against the November rain. In Norway, people would be home, having supper at this hour. But here there was business to be done. And not only by men. Young women stood on street corners, talking with sailors. Children loaded stalls.

'Oranges from Seville!'

'Hot chestnuts!'

'Spiced Jamaican rum!'

Mountain-man bought me and Morten an orange each, a bag of chestnuts to share and a spiced rum for himself. He drank it and bought another. We used our knives to cut the oranges. A strange fruit, like a small sun.

Mountain-man led the way, cutting through the crowd like a ship through waves. And we followed.

I had to keep a good track on him, because there was so much to see. The English themselves were most interesting. Paler and shorter than Norwegians. I'm not sure how they conquered the world.

One girl (pretty) smiled and spoke to me. I don't speak any English, so I didn't understand. I smiled too (she was very pretty!). But Mountain-man came and grabbed me by the scruff and hurried me on.

'What did she say?' I asked.

'She said she has been to church and had a lovely time.'

But Morten told me after she'd said, 'Look at your hair, boy. I never seen such. Like hay in the sun!'

As I say, there was lots of skinny, pasty English, but there were others too. Sailors, whalers, traders of every colour and country I've been told about and seen in magazines. Lots had tattoos: pictures of girls, whales and ships on their forearms and hands. Blue ink swallows, which, Mountain-man told me, will take a sailor's soul to heaven if they go down with their ship. One man even had an anchor inked on his right cheek.

We followed Mountain-man along cobbled streets, past houses and factories, packed tight like trees in the darkest part of a forest, through a maze of alleys and into a square with a lot of taverns and stores around its edges. Mountain-man stood in the centre of the square and held his arms wide like a circus master.

'What do you think?'

'It's amazing,' I said.

'Is this what you wanted to show us?' said Morten, crossing his arms.

'Yes, but not only the city. This is part of your education.'

'I see, Mr Olufsen,' I said. But in truth I didn't know what he was talking about.

'Do you know why God gave us the whale, boys?'

I couldn't see what this city and hunting whales had to do with each other, but I didn't say.

Mountain-man carried on. 'Did you ever consider what happens to the whale, after we kill it?'

'Factory ship takes it,' said Morten. 'Or it goes to the station on Deception Island. We have the meat and oil; freeze one, put the other in barrels, save the bones too. Take it all home to Norway, where the oil is refined.'

But Morten missed a lot out. What about the time between the kill and the boxes and barrels? It's odd to think of the giant beast, and what is in those boxes and barrels unloaded at Tonsberg dock, and believe they are the same thing.

'Does it take long, to… process?' I said.

'No. The factory ship will find us after the kill. They winch her, then the boys work, like ants on a bowl of blueberries. Flence her, cut her up, freeze and pack the meat. You will not believe how fast. And we will feast on the tongue.' He patted his considerable gut. He looked like a whale himself. Huge and grand. But no one would feast on *his* tongue.

'Oil, fat, bones, meat,' said the Mountain-man. 'All good for something. Nothing goes back in the sea. Nothing. And then?'

'We sell it to the English,' Morten said.

'And what do they do with it?'

Morten shrugged. 'Eat it?'

'You see that factory?' said Mountain-man. He pointed down a side street to a square building, with high walls and iron gates. 'The machines inside are greased with whale fat.

'You see that woman? You think she is really shaped like an hourglass? The corset that squeezes her is made of whalebone.

'You see the Englishman too soft to walk in the rain, the spines of his umbrella are whale bone too. The springs in the typewriter, that certified our shore-leave papers. The keys in that tavern's piano, knocking out that awful noise. The candles in that window. The soap these people wash with. The lamps that shone in the night before electricity.'

The streetlamps lit the city like candles on a

Christmas tree. How much oil had *that* taken? Night after night, year after year.

'All whale, boys,' said Mountain-man. 'Flesh and bone and oil.' He pulled his watch from his pocket, opened its casing and showed it to us. The tiny workings whirred round and round. How can any machine be so small yet track time like it does? Why do I ask such questions? I don't know. Mor says I have too much curiosity. And that's what killed the cat, apparently.

'Look at the cogs.' Mountain-man rubbed his fingers together. 'So delicate, only whale oil can grease the workings of this watch. Cities run on fuel, like a train's furnace runs on coal. Here the fuel has been the whale, for two hundred years and longer. Not only this city, many of them. *This* is why we do what we do.'

'How many?' I said. Because, again, I cannot help asking such questions.

'How many what?'

'How many whales must we kill, to keep this... watch working?'

'Ach,' Mountain-man scratched his head. 'Between us, the Americans and English. Millions.'

I couldn't imagine it. 'If we take millions, are there millions more in the sea to be killed?' I said.

Mountain-man laughed. 'God gave us a bountiful sea, Peer. You have seen only the smallest piece. How big do you think it is?'

'True, Mr Olufsen, yes. But millions?'

'There are more whales than we could ever hunt and...' He pulled a hand to his face, pointed a finger and looked down it, as though it was the sight of a gun. 'I am the man who will hunt them.'

'I'm going to be a gunner, one day,' Morten said. 'Let me pull the trigger on the first kill.'

It was a tradition in those days. A boy fired the harpoon on the first shot of the season, with some help from the gunner. If the shot hit, it was a good omen.

'Of *course* you want to be a gunner,' said Mountain-man. 'I make more money than the captain! But Sven is marked for it. You will make soup and scrub decks a few years before you get *that* chance.'

'I'd be good,' said Morten, chest out, proud as a cockerel. 'I can shoot. I killed a deer once.'

'Oh,' I said. 'You never told me *that* before.'

Mountain-man folded his thick arms across his chest and raised an eyebrow. 'You shoot a deer when it stops still and you are standing on solid earth. It is different hitting a moving beast from a moving boat.'

'But the whale is so big,' Morten said.

'Yes, but you must shoot it here.' Mountain-man unfolded his arms and tapped the nape of my neck, with a finger the size of a sausage. 'The target is no bigger than a tablecloth. The time no more than a second before the whale dives.'

'I have the eye. The hand too!' said Morten. 'You've seen me with a catapult.'

We had brought our catapults on the voyage. We stole a lot of dried peas and hazelnuts from the store for ammunition, until the captain banned us. But Morten still had his weapon and he carried it everywhere.

'Hold this.' Morten thrust his bag of chestnuts into my hand, then pulled the catapult from his back pocket. 'Want to see?'

'See what?' I said.

'See me hit something. Make it hard too,' he said, grinning like a madman.

'Okay,' said Mountain-man, 'hit that.' He pointed to a street sign, high on a wall on the corner of the square.

'Too easy,' I said.

'You got a better idea?' said Morten.

'The man on that balcony, up there?'

'Wearing the apron, smoking a pipe?'

'Yes. He is a big target, but he is far. Like a whale.'

I waited for Morten's stupid grin to vanish. But it didn't. He raised the catapult.

'Stop,' said Mountain-man, pushing Morten's hand down. 'I can't approve of such an outrage. I mean… you don't want him to see you.'

We waited till the man turned and leaned over the far end of the balcony, banging his pipe against the wall to empty it.

Morten grabbed a chestnut, took aim and fired. It hit the man smack on his right bum cheek. The man reared up like a bee-stung horse.

We turned away and huddled in a tight circle, as if we were deep in conversation.

'Who threw that?' the man yelled.

'What did he say, what's he doing?' I whispered.

Mountain-man looked over my shoulder, but he couldn't answer. His shoulders trembled as he tried not to laugh. When he got control of himself, he spluttered, 'That was a hell of a shot.'

I have to admit it, I was jealous. So I blurted out, 'I can do better.'

Only four words, but look what they led to.

Morten took the bag of nuts and handed me the catapult.

'Perhaps a moving target,' he said. 'How about him?' Morten pointed at the man we'd seen before, the one with the umbrella. Now the rain had stopped, he'd put the umbrella down and I saw he wore a Homburg hat. He was walking away from the square.

I looked at Mountain-man, he nodded.

'Be fast about it. The longer you wait, the further he will go.'

I grabbed a nut. It was a lumpy, awkward shape and too light, and that would make the shot tricky. But there was no time to choose another. I took aim, and all the time Morten's eyes bored into me like a drill.

The nut flew high, arced, and knocked the hat clean off the man's head. Baffled, he looked around, then picked up his hat, put it on and carried on walking.

CHRIS VICK

'Good,' said Mountain-man, nodding and stroking his beard.

'Let me,' Morten said. 'First shot of the season. I asked first. The lucky shot.'

Mountain-man shook his head. 'I told you, it's Sven. This is his third season, you must be patient.'

'But next year,' Morten said. His eyes were hungry. He was like a dog after a bone.

'What about you, Peer? You have a good eye.'

'Yes. I want to shoot the harpoon.' Now I think on it, I spoke the words before I'd even thought them. Morten wanted it, and it was something valuable and important. So of course, I wanted it too.

Peer the gunner, I wondered. Was it possible? It would take years. But to kill a whale? Me?

'You sure, boy?' said Mountain-man. 'You look like you just decided to jump off a cliff.'

Now I *did* think. Mor was pregnant again. I would have a half-sister or brother soon enough and we would need money.

I tried to imagine standing on the prow, finger on the trigger and the whole crew's eyes on me. I tried to imagine the great beast, its mighty head rising from the broiling water. And the explosion as the harpoon fired. The beast slowing. The water turning red. I tried to imagine it. But the closest I'd come to a whale was those boxes and barrels streaming onto the dockside, when the ships returned in the spring.

I thought a whole lot of things then, I felt a whole

lot of things. But all that came out my mouth was, 'Yes, I am sure.'

'But you can't both do it, so...' Mountain-man took a coin from his pocket. 'An English shilling I should have spent in a tavern by now. Heads it is Peer, tails, Morten. Whoever wins, next year, or maybe the year after, he gets to pull the trigger.'

Morten stared at me, amazed. Had the gunner *really* made that promise, here and now? Maybe he really was impressed with our shooting. Maybe it was the two rums.

Mountain-man flipped the coin. It spun, twinkling and glittering in the streetlight. He caught it and slapped it on the back of his left hand. We leaned in.

'Heads.'

I looked close, to be certain. The king of England stared back at me.

'Best of three?' Morten said.

'No chance.'

One day, I, Peer would fire the harpoon. And that was that.

Mountain-man gave me the coin. 'Keep it. A reminder of my promise.'

I held it in my palm. I couldn't stop staring at it.

'Anything to say?' said Mountain-man.

I didn't know *what* to say.

'Um, thank you.'

The gunner took out his pocket watch, with its tiny workings, greased with whale oil.

'Okay, let's walk. I want you to see more of this place before leave is over.' Mountain-man walked off and Morten glared at me, his face dark as a storm cloud.

'You haven't the guts. You won't do it.'

'I have,' I said. 'I will.'

 ## The Ross Sea – the day before

I stumbled across the deck, hammered by wind and rain, trying to carry a hunk of bread and a cup of soup. Each time the boat lurched, slops of liquid scorched my hand.

That sly cook-boy Morten had filled the cup to the brim. He *wanted* me to spill it, or maybe drop the cup. To look a fool anyhow. But I refused to be that fool, no matter how bad the burning. I tried to steady myself, but I didn't have sea-legs and staggered and swayed like a drunk, burning my fingers, leaving a trail of soupy splodges.

The gunner stood at the prow with his hand on the harpoon cannon, his body covered by a black oilskin coat. His beard and the woollen hat hid most of his face – all I could see were his coal eyes, staring steady out to sea.

As I reached him the boat dipped into a trough. I slipped, half-fell, righted myself. By now most of the soup was on the deck. I would have to get more. How Morten would laugh.

'Here you are, Mr Olufsen.'

'Thank you, boy... what! Less than half?'

'Sorry, Mr Olufsen.'

'Ah, you are fresh. No matter.' Mountain-man scoffed the bread and soup and wiped his beard clean on his sleeve, then took position again. His eyes glazed over as if they were not looking at all. Or seeing something I could not.

I've seen that look before, of course. In the eyes of men before the ships sailed, when they paced the docks and drained the bars and got in fights. When the men got that way the women could not wait for them to leave.

What is it that makes men swap the green mountains of Norway for this? Endless hills of grey water that come from nowhere and go nowhere. What makes them travel halfway round the wide world to kill whales? Is it money? I had an uncle in Oslo, who sold insurance and had a good life. I knew farmers and shopkeepers too. They didn't have this look. Only the men who went to sea had it.

I was fourteen. I was one of them. At sea for no reason other than because it was expected, not because I chose it. I thought, perhaps when I see a whale, when I kill one, I will know why they look that way. Perhaps in time I'll be the same.

'Are you searching the sea for whales?' I asked.

'No. That's his job.' Mountain-man nodded skyward, to the crow's nest. There was the seeker, crammed like a sardine in a can, wrapped in furs and wool, his binoculars glued to his face. He looked more creature than man and the binoculars were his eyes.

'So what are you looking for?' I said. Mountain-man woke from his dream then and from inside his coat he took a leather-coated flask. He drank then handed it to me.

I looked around.

'Drinking is not allowed,' I said.

'I am the gunner,' said Mountain-man with a wink. I took a swig. I didn't like it much, but it warmed my belly better than soup.

'The sea is my refuge,' said Mountain-man. 'Like the church is your mother's. We all need somewhere, boy.'

'But a church is a safe place.'

A wave roared as the ship lunged into it. Mountain-man had to grab me to stop me falling. He half-shouted then, to be heard above the wind.

'You know, when we've been out months, we long for home. Dry land, fresh meat, aquavit – and to see our wives and children. I have seen men go crazy wanting home. But here is the truth. When we have seen summer fade and the days get shorter and the air colder. *Then*, the autumn is a fog in our hearts and it is all I can do to stop myself punching people. *Then...*' he wagged a finger, 'it is time to get to sea, boy. Just so I can bloody breathe!' He guffawed. 'Peer. There is freedom out here if you want to find it.'

'Yes, Mr Olufsen.'

I wished right then I felt what Mountain-man felt. But the whole journey south I'd been seasick or homesick or both and I didn't know why I was there, or if it was where I should be. But I had that coin in my pocket, didn't I? And maybe that was the answer.

It was spring, coming into summer there. But it was not like Norwegian summers. No warm sunset, no cloudberries, no trout fishing and fires, no deer, or forest. Hardly a bird in the sky. Only grey sea and sky, and the days colder with every latitude we crossed. Some summer!

And we had not seen a whale.

Here we were, a dozen crew on the gunner boat, far from the factory ship, bobbing like a fish float, zigzagging, searching. On and on.

'Will we *ever* find a whale?' I asked.

And then, right then, no more than a second later, I swear it is true—

'There she blows!' the seeker cried.

'God was listening to you,' Mountain-man said.

The seeker dropped his binoculars and pointed to the starboard horizon. Mountain-man's head turned, eyes eagle-sharp.

I went starboard and searched, not only with my eyes, with my heart too. Was it there, finally? A whale.

Men rushed from the engine house, up from the hold and galley. Morten came last in his apron, still carrying a ladle. The crew lined the starboard. They looked up to the seeker, once, twice more, checking their sight against the compass needle of his arm. An arrow to the hunt.

A distant blur of a grey island appeared in the water, then sank from view.

My heart beat like a drum. I shook. Around me hungry faces, men standing on tiptoe, craning to see, hands pointing, filling the air with excited shouts.

We looked for another blow and waited for the seeker's cry.

Seconds passed like hours. But all I could see was shifting peaks and wind-blown crests.

Then—

'She blows again!'

A faint plume, mist-breath, in the far distance.

The slightest sign.

But enough.

The crew rushed around. Some to the engine room, some below, to fetch harpoons and ropes.

The engine roared. The boat swung, plunging in the waves, churning through walls of water.

The spray of breath. Closer.

'The whale comes at us!' Mountain-man shouted. 'Dead on!'

Its grey back broke the surface, like an island being born, and rose and rose an – *phoosh!* – the breath, a cloud of mist, and an arcing hill that got bigger and bigger and bigger.

It was *huge*!

The back went under and the fluke rose above the waves. The tail shaped like bird's wings, wide as a house.

'My God!' I shouted.

Men carrying harpoons and rope struggled on the rocking deck.

'Are you sleeping?' Mountain-man roared. 'She'll be under and away, load the cannon!'

It was all happening in a split second. And would Sven pull the trigger? Where was he?

The whale showed again – bigger than any boat and faster too – then vanished.

Mountain-man waved to the engine room. He swiped a hand across his throat. The signal.

'Cut the engine!'

The men busied themselves. But as they loaded the weapon, a great shadow was in the water ahead of us, blue and grey, flecked with white. Ten times bigger than the gunboat. And from beneath we heard a throbbing, moaning, haunting song.

'What is that? What is it?' I said.

'The whale, of course,' Mountain-man said.

The shadow passed under the boat. A moving grey-blue island. Graceful, powerful, slick, silent now. And I felt as if I was floating, un-anchored from the world.

The engine slowed to a gentle throb, leaving the boat rocking, uselessly, in the waves. Everyone looked to Mountain-man. Whatever he said, we would do. But he only put his hands on his hips and shook his head. 'It's over for now.'

'Will we not chase it?' I asked.

'This one is fast. You feel that against the hull, from behind us. The swell. We will not catch the whale now. Wherever she's going, she's in a hurry. When a whale moves like this, we need to be very quick or very lucky. But we can follow. It may take hours, but the hunt has begun. She cannot swim that fast so far.'

I went aft. The hunger to see this giant beast again was like nothing I'd ever known. The whale was like nothing I'd ever seen.

I examined the harpoon with its iron arrow point – the size of a man's head – and the shaft, and the long rope that tethers the body of the whale to the boat. I tried to imagine firing the harpoon, to see in my mind the arrow finding its target, and the reloading and the firing again, and the whale slowing as its life drained into the water. How much blood is in that thing? How red will the water turn? How long, till it has no more fight, and is dead? Till it has lost and we have won.

 The Ross Sea. The hunt.

We chased the whale half an hour or more through strengthening winds and surging waves.

Sitting in the dark of the hold, I imagined the boat was alive, sweating and grunting steadily towards the fleeing whale. It reminded me, strangely, of running through wet wheat; the sea and wind pushing and pulling us, this way and that.

The boat was strong, though, and the engine was in full throttle. She heaved forward, rising and falling to the sea's rhythm.

Everyone was busy. I told myself I'd go on deck soon. I knew I should want to, but I sat at the table with Mountain-man, a hand inside my pocket, rubbing and squeezing the coin.

'How do you feel?' Mountain-man said. 'Next year it might be you, not Sven.'

'Good,' I said. I'd see a dozen whales killed before then. More.

I'd see Morten cook whale meat. I would eat it and, like all of them, be glad not to sup on fish or dry, salted meat.

'Sven!' Mountain-man shouted. 'Where are you? It's time, boy.'

Mountain-man was excited. I heard it, saw it in his twinkling eyes and massive hand drumming the table.

The door to the bunkroom swung open. Sven staggered out, clutching his stomach with one hand and a bucket with the other.

He swayed to the table and sat.

The hold emptied of men rushing to deck, leaving me, Sven and Mountain-man.

'Seasick, Sven,' said Mountain-man.

Sven nodded, then made good use of the bucket.

'Get it all out, boy,' Mountain-man thumped Sven between his shoulders, 'then come on deck and kill a whale.'

An empty shell of a boy looked up, drained of everything that was once Sven. His hair hung lank and damp around his face. He looked drowned. A ghost of a boy.

'Have a drink,' Mountain-man said. 'Settle your guts.'

'Don't make me do this,' Sven said. This ghost had eyes alive enough to plead.

'You want to, no?'

Sven dipped his face over the bucket. He wasn't sick, but he didn't look up again either. He shook his head.

The door to the stairs swung open. It was Morten.

'Captain says, get on deck. We're almost on the whale. I've seen it, Peer. A monster! What you waiting for? Come and see. You too, Sven, come on!

Morten was the opposite of Sven, more alive than I'd ever seen him.

Mountain-man stood, picked up Sven, and carried him like a ragdoll to the bunkroom, returning alone.

'No matter. He can kill another whale, in calmer waters. Tell the captain I'll be up soon.'

'But the coin, your promise!' Morten said. 'A boy must pull the trigger. It's for luck. Peer *must* pull the trigger. I'll tell the others.'

Before I could say anything, before I could even think, Morten turned and vanished.

'Well?' Mountain-man said. I nodded. But right there and then I was a ghost-boy too.

That was when I drank the glass of aquavit. After the ice and fire I got up, floating, dreaming. I started to walk and glancing behind, half-expected to see my body still sitting at the table.

I followed Mountain-man, wishing I could be like him, so sure, so strong. To have killed a dozen whales. A hundred. To know this is nothing, something everyday, easy as eating stew, or scrubbing decks.

As I climbed the steps, a memory crashed into my mind.

The summer before Papa died, I shot a hare with my catapult. It caught the hare in the leg, wounding but not killing it. The thing limped away to hide. I remember Papa raising his rifle and the crack of the shot echoing through the valley. How the hare fell, how I ran to it, in time to watch the light fade in its eyes.

I didn't like that much. It made me sad, though I hid that from Papa.

I killed more hares after that. It became normal. And I scoffed at Greta in her fancy pigtails and summer dress, when she said hunting was disgusting, as she gorged on a pork sausage that someone else had been kind enough to kill and gut and pack up for her to eat.

So I know what it is to kill.

I gripped the rope on the bannister, and forced my hand to haul my body, because it didn't want to move.

Somehow, I made my way on deck.

A shower of salt spray stung my face. A rush of chill air woke me from my dead dream. The boat rocked and swung, dancing giddily in waves and wind.

And there was Morten, with wide, glaring eyes and a lunatic grin.

'*This* I want to see,' he said.

The captain whacked me on the shoulder and laughed. 'You have no chance of hitting the whale in seas like this. It's just for fun – a tradition, you know. Hit or miss, Peer, it doesn't matter.'

But Mountain-man was waiting too.

'We will not miss!'

Mountain-man used his sea-legs to find a path across the rolling deck and I followed; a duckling, waddling behind its mother.

'She blows! She comes again,' the seeker cried. But all I could see was slate-grey sea.

But then, there – a plume of breath before she dived. And now we could follow the pattern of diving and surfacing.

Mountain-man got hold of the trigger end of the harpoon. But he did not aim. Not yet. He looked to the seeker, made hand signals of waves and cuts to the captain who watched from the window of the wheel room. Mountain-man shouted, 'Speed up,' then, seconds later, 'Slow down.'

It seemed like a dance of waves and wind and ship, of gunner, seeker and captain.

The whale was in front, a hundred metres off the bow. And I was at the cannon. Mountain-man guided my hands, one holding the handle, the other on the trigger.

Only then did I notice the harpoon was already loaded. The arrowhead ready.

When he was sure I was set right, Mountain-man said, 'Keep your finger tight, but do not pull.'

I stood with legs wide apart to keep stable. Mountain-man moved around me and held the cannon and swung the weight of it left then right, up, down, keeping it true to the whale's shadow.

I was part of the dance and the music would not stop until the whale was dead.

Twenty metres ahead the shade of white rose from the green depths. Mountain-man aimed.

'Ready for her?'

The whale broke the surface, breathed and sank. Mountain-man manoeuvred the cannon, somehow seeing where the whale was, even when she was not visible.

'The next time she is up, I will shout and you will shoot,' he said.

'How do you know it's a she?'

'She is big. She is pregnant.'

'Pregnant?'

'She rises!' the seeker cried.

I saw the whale.

I gripped tight. All of me – my whole being – ran like a river, down my arm, into my hand, into my finger.

The captain, seeker, Morten, Mountain-man, the crew. Watching.

'Do it!' Morten cried.

I tried to imagine the harpoon was a catapult. Brain, eye and hand working together.

The whale came again, a moving, rising mountain. She slowed.

'Your mother would be proud,' said Mountain-man.

There she was, in my mind, Mor, rubbing her growing belly.

I told myself I was ready.

I swear I could feel the whale's exhaustion. And told myself it was kinder, now, to shoot.

'Pull the trigger when I say,' Mountain-man said.

'Yes.'

'Are you ready?'

But there, in my mind, the dying hare again. Unasked for, unexpected. And the light fading in its amber eyes.

'No.'

'What?'

'I don't want to do it, Mr Olufsen.'

I turned and looked at Mountain-man. And the gunner looked back, exactly like the priest at the church gate looked at me, right before Papa's funeral.

'You must,' Mountain-man said, gently, in my ear.

I shook my head. Mountain-man looked to the kill-hungry crew.

'Do you trust me?'

'Yes.'

'Then shoot when I say.'

'But... I told you already... I don't want to.'

'I hear you, boy, I hear you. Now trust me.'

The seeker shouted, 'She comes again!'

She rose and broke the surface. The ship was almost on top of her. I braced, expecting the hull to collide with the whale.

My finger was on the trigger. Mountain-man looked down the sight at the back of the whale's head.

'Ready,' he shouted, and moved the cannon. A nudge to the left – enough to change the shot.

'Now!' Mountain-man shouted.

I pulled the trigger and the harpoon exploded from the cannon. The pile of coiled rope unravelled at furious speed. The harpoon arced. The arrowhead bounced, cut and grazed the flesh on the whale's head, then landed in the grey sea, where it sank, harmless as a thrown anchor. The whale breathed and dived, leaving a cloud of blood in the water.

'Reload! Reload!' the captain screamed from the wheelhouse.

Mountain-man let go of the cannon. He turned to face the captain, running out of the wheelhouse.

Mountain-man shook his head.

'We are hunting, Olufsen. The ship wants a kill.'

'Then find another whale and call me when you want me to kill it. There'll be others near. That's my bet and you'll see I'm right. We're on them now, time to kill as many as we like.'

The seeker scanned the waves, training his binoculars on the horizon.

'There they blow!' he cried.

All heads turned. The distant horizon filled with plume-cloud breaths.

'Minke whales,' said Mountain-man. 'Smaller, not so smart. It will be a while before we reach them in these seas. But we *will* reach them, so no need to chase this one.'

'You had better be right,' the captain said.

'I am. Now come on, Peer, let's go and drink some of that wonderful Venezuelan coffee.' He put his arm around my shoulder, and walked me away, guiding me, in the same way he had guided the cannon.

'Well done,' he said, squeezing my shoulder tight, like a vice.

'But we missed. *I* missed.'

'Did we?' There was mischief in the giant's eyes.

'The whale was in our sights, Mr Olufsen. It would have been easy.' I didn't know if I was trying to convince Mountain-man or myself.

'No, boy. It wouldn't. Not if your heart was not in it.'

 After

We sat at the table. Sven's moans echoed from the bunkroom.

It was as though it hadn't happened. As though we were just now waiting to be called.

Morten followed us down. Of course he did.

I remember gazing at the table, the intricate grain of the wood.

'Will you make me coffee, Morten?' said Mountain-man. 'And some soup. For Peer too.'

'Soup?' I said. The word sounded foreign, it had no meaning.

Morten didn't go to make soup, he stood in front of us, arms folded.

'What happened?'

'I missed.'

'Yes, you did, didn't you?'

'Soup and coffee,' Mountain-man said. 'If it's not too much trouble for the galley boy.'

'The ship is rising and falling,' Morten said. 'I can't make soup now, we're not steady enough.'

'Then coffee.'

'But…'

One glance from Mountain-man shut him up.

Morten ground the beans, then boiled the grounds. The hold filled with the thick aroma of coffee. Over minutes the swell and winds eased. By the time the coffee was served the boat was on an even keel.

'I thought maybe we were in for a storm,' said Mountain-man. 'But it was only a squall.'

The boat chugged steadily along. Mountain-man took noisy sips of coffee.

'Good,' he said, 'now the soup.'

Morten shuffled to the stove, found vegetables and a knife and set about cooking stock.

'I saw,' Morten said.

'What did you see?' Mountain-man said.

I knew what Morten saw.

'You moved the cannon at the last second. You missed on purpose. Are you a coward?'

I got up and stood in front of Morten. The cooking table was a barrier between us. He stared at me. I was thinking of leaning over and punching him, and I know he was thinking of doing the same to me. Getting one in first.

'I am not a coward,' I said. After a few seconds he carried on chopping and cutting.

'Are you going to help me cook, then?' said Morten, who seemed unsettled by me, so close.

'Give me the ladle and your apron,' I said

'What?'

'Give me the ladle and your apron.'

'No.'

'You want to kill a whale? Go and sit with Mr Olufsen and drink coffee. Get yourself ready.'

'They will call me soon,' said Mountain-man. 'They will expect Peer to have another go. But no one will mind if it is you.'

Morten wiped his hands on the apron, undid it and handed it to me. He went and sat with Mountain-man and I went to the chiller and took out a fish.

'I'll cook.' I chopped the vegetables, more finely than Morten had. I sliced an onion and put it in a pan with oil and set it on the stove. Then I took herbs from a jar and sprinkled some in.

'Did you know this dried dill was here, Morten?'

Morten and Mountain-man sat in silence, watching. As the herbs and onion began to cook, I started on the fish with a knife.

Sven came out from the bunkroom.

'What's that?' he said, sniffing the air.

'Stew.' I added the vegetables to the mix, then water. Fish heads, whole onions, peppercorns.

'I don't want to eat fish heads and onions,' Morten said.

'You won't, they are only for the stock. This is how much salt you use.' I sprinkled some in. 'You don't throw it in like a handful of snow.'

'I can cook,' Morten said.

'No, you can't. You leave the fish bones in too long. You make the stock bitter. And you don't boil the stock down slowly or long enough. You want to kill a whale, Morten? Go ahead. I'll cook.'

Morten sat, grinning, but nervy, like an angry dog.

'You're a coward,' he barked.

Mountain-man raised a hand and Morten flinched. The gunner paused, his hand in the air, but after a moment watching Morten, lowered his arm and put his hand in his pocket.

'Ach, you are not worth it.'

14

The Letter

'Why have you stopped reading, Bestemor?' Abi asks.

'The light. It is not so good. And I am tired. It is not easy to do this; to read and translate also.'

'But there's more?'

Bestemor flicks through the pages, pausing on some, riffling through others.

'Seems he was not quite the murderer you thought, Abi.'

'No, I guess... I mean, he *was* a whaler, though. He did work on those ships.'

'You would have done differently, I suppose?'

'Of course!'

'You cannot know that, Abigail. You have knowledge, you have education. But they did not. They did not know what the whale was, not really.'

'Sure. He made a choice, a good choice, I get that, but...' Abi struggles to find the words, the *thoughts*. 'My poor brain can't compute this. It's... it's...'

'Complicated? Certainty on such matters is a luxury.'

'What does the rest say – what's in there?'

'From the bits I read it is about the later times. He must have bought the taping equipment in Norway. My mother was so disappointed in him. She never understood how Morten became a gunner – and not Papa. Why he had settled for being a cook. Not a bad way to earn money, he became quite famous for it. Captains used to bid for him to travel on their ships. But the money was nothing compared to being the seeker, captain or gunner. He was careful, though, he bought shares in the whaling company, and later oil. This explains so much.'

'What does he say about the recordings?'

'I am chilly. Let's go inside. I'll make you a deal. You finish off the cooking, I will light the oil lamp and read from the book. Okay?' Bestemor holds out her hand, and Abi shakes it. Her grandmother's hand is rough on the palm and fingers, but soft on top. It feels fragile.

There is a front room, with a table and two chairs at one end and the kitchen at the other. Taps and a sink. Two chests for storage. A stove. A wood burner. By the burner is an open door to the cottage's only other room, where Bestemor sleeps. Abi looks in.

A reindeer's skull and antlers hang on the wall; a tree branch of bone, yellow with age. A fur, possibly from the same animal, lies on the floor in front of another log burner. The room smells of pine, mingling with the aroma of the stew. Abi's mouth waters. She follows the smell to the 'kitchen'.

'Taste it, see what it needs,' Bestemor says, 'then put a log in the stove fire.' She sits in an armchair by the wood burner, and pokes at the embers with a stick, blows on them, stokes them with dry moss and twigs she takes from a fireside basket.

'Strange the paths people take in life. And why. These recordings. So many. An obsession. Yet I do not think Papa did anything with them.'

Abi stirs and tastes. She adds pepper, more salt, some wine.

Bestemor – once she is satisfied the fire is going – lights the lamp and reads the notes, flicking through the pages.

'I'll say if there's anything worth mentioning. But this part seems to be about the whales – their numbers, how they behave – but in the later part there is even more detail, in such fine writing. Here he records the numbers of whaling ships. There he talks only of shoals of fish: what type, what direction they seem to be moving. And the plankton too, the food of the great whales. And here... oh—' Bestemor hesitates.

From the pages of the notebook she pulls an envelope, which she opens.

'It is a letter from Papa, to the university in Oslo. He introduces himself, and says he has findings that may be of interest. He tells of the recordings.'

'What does it say?'

'This: *I have, after many years, made conclusions about the language and songs of the great whales. Their communication can be categorised in two ways.*

'*The first type appears in short bursts of whistles, clicks and moans. I take this to be some kind of language, communicating – as so many animals do – about imminent danger, or the location and abundance of food. I have heard particular phrases used when mothers call to calves and vice versa. It is as though they have names. I have heard them use other phrases and seen them gather as they follow shoals of fish and clouds of plankton.*

'*It is impossible to decipher completely. It is similar to the language of other animals, only more complex. A language perhaps surpassed only by our own.*

'*The second type, the songs pertaining to some species, are altogether more sophisticated. It is these that I have studied, and in attempting to decipher them I am pleading for your help.*

'*What can I say with any authority?*

'*To begin with, the song as much as the sight of the whale is impressive. They last half an hour or more. The amount and complexity of information is similar to that of a complete symphony, or perhaps a very long, very detailed book.*

'*These songs rarely correspond with sightings. For the most part, when we see the whales we do not hear their songs, and when we hear them we do not see the whales.*

'*There is basic structure, but otherwise much variety. It was with some shock that, after a period of study, I found that one song, recorded near to home, was almost identical to another I had recorded in Antarctica.*

'Perhaps the same whale had travelled a very long way? Yet on sighting the whale singing – a rarity, and blind luck that I had observed both singers of this song – I deduced it was not. Their markings were quite different. Perhaps one whale had passed the song to another that had travelled?

'With further study I found the whale near Norway was what scientists call resident, rather than transitory or migratory. It was, you see, the song that had travelled, not the whale.

'I reflected on this for many months, and in that time listened to many recordings. A pattern emerged. The content of the songs corresponded with weather, sea temperature, certain notes with numbers of whales that I observed in the days after, with herring shoals, and more. On further voyages I made notes about not only the whales, but all environmental information.

'My conclusion? I believe the songs are – in effect – a song, morphed into ever-changing symphonies, sung by an ever-changing chorus. But they are more than that. They are, if you will, a telegraph of information, a network of whale minds.

'Is this such a leap of imagination? Their brains are huge, not only as an aspect of their size – many dinosaurs had brains the size of walnuts – but for what evolutionary purpose? This is not simply a question of intelligence. There is a community, one meta community

*of whales, which appears to record and mirror the status
of the ocean.*

'But how can I find evidence for this?

*'It would take a mind – or minds – much greater than
mine. It would take many recordings, corresponding
with sightings and other information to even explore this
theory, let alone evidence it.*

*'So, to come to the purpose of my letter. I respectfully
request your help in this matter – to place observers and
recording equipment on more whaling vessels.*

*'I appreciate this is an unorthodox request, but I
urge you to listen to the recordings yourself, to read
my notes and observations. And for a meeting to
discuss my proposal.*

'Yours faithfully, Peer Kristensen.'

*'PS. I do not know precisely the true nature of
these songs. Yet I feel in my heart, it is perhaps even
richer and stranger, than I imagine.'*

Bestemor places the letter on her lap.

'He never sent it, did he?' Abi says.

'Oh, he sent it. The address on the envelope is ours.
But it is not in his writing. It seems to me, the letter was
returned to him, with no reply. Now, I think I understand
why he didn't speak too much of this work.'

'Why? Why didn't they reply?' Abi says. 'Why weren't
they interested?'

'This country is a whaling nation even now, but once
it was almost our entire industry. What Norwegian

professor in that time would research whales in this way? What benefit could there be to him? To make himself a pariah. The only interest they had then was finding new and better ways to kill whales, to process and sell them.

'It was other people – Americans, I think – who did the research in the 1960s and 70s, finding the evidence that later made almost all countries stop the dreadful hunt. Not us, though.'

'Wow. Not a murderer at all, then. Not really. He *knew* there was something special about them. He just never got the chance to prove it. That's so sad.'

'The world and whales must wait while we have supper. I think you need to take the stock off the stove. And perhaps go and inform our family that supper is almost ready. It might be a way for you to get back in your folks' good books!'

Abi wipes her hands on the apron, takes it off and goes outside. It has stopped raining. The sky is clearing. She can see the horizon once again. She begins to walk up the hill, but pauses, as she does so many times on the island, simply to turn and look at the sea.

'Oh, Moonlight. I'm sure you could make sense of...' She is about to say 'the songs', but stops, and thinks. Of the letter. The notebooks. The tapes. Of Moonlight's observations. She turns and runs down the hill, bursting into the cottage.

'It's like Moonlight said, and great-grandfather Peer too – one song, or many, or a symphony, but played by lots of different instruments, as though the whales are an orchestra, but so is the sea itself, and everything that lives in it! And Peer too!'

'You are talking crazy, calm down!' said Bestemor.

'Whales migrate, right? But how do they know where to go? And more importantly, what if they knew what was waiting for them, not only on the journey, but at its end. Peer said a "telegraph" of information. And… and…'

'Yes?'

'Bestemor. They're not songs at all. Not really.'

'Then what are they?'

Abi stands at the door, her eyes fixed on the sea. 'They are a lot of things, but if I had to say what in one word… they're *maps*, Bestemor… They're maps.'

15

Searching

Before the house has woken, Abi stands on the shore with Bestemor.

A canoe lies at the water's edge. Inside are two lifejackets, a snorkel, flippers, towels, a picnic basket, the wide-brimmed hat Bestemor gave her and an anchor and rope.

With occasional glances at the house, they put on the lifejackets.

'Hurry,' Bestemor says. 'Before anyone's up. And you'll have to pull this thing into the water, I don't have the strength.'

'Are you sure, I mean… I'm grounded, aren't I? It's not like swimming to Hvalryggøy. They're going to see us. Dad's going to go mental.'

Bestemor rolls her eyes. 'You did a stupid thing before. It was dangerous. Is it dangerous now? The sea is calm. Will you forget lifejackets now? No. Are you

CHRIS VICK

alone, or putting your sister in danger? No. You think
it is as simple as disobeying your father in all things one
day, then doing exactly what he tells you the next? You
are not really thinking, are you? And if we are sent to the
doghouse, at least we'll go together. The cottage is a nice
doghouse. What can they do to you, Abi?'

Abi opens her arms and hurls herself at Bestemor.

'Don't squeeze me so tight, I am not a grapefruit.'

Abi tries to guess – to *remember* where the whales had
appeared when the squall hit. But today the sea is as featureless as it is limitless. When they are some way out,
when the islands, the house, the hut all look roughly the
same size as she thinks they did in the storm, they stop
paddling and sink the anchor.

What had Moonlight said?

'I am waterproof to a depth of fifteen metres.'
Something like that.

'Here.' Bestemor shakes the snorkel mask at Abi.

Abi unstraps her lifejacket. She imagines swimming
down. Underwater.

In an instant she's gripping the side of the canoe. Her
breath speeds up. It's in her throat. She struggles for air,
sweats.

'Abi— Abigail!' Bestemor looks at her with great
concern.

'I'm okay, I just… I don't know if I can do it.' She tries

to get hold of her breath. Remembers her EC training. 'Bit panicky, that's all.'

'We have all the time in the world. Here is an idea: why don't you start by leaning over and putting only your face in the water, with the snorkel on.'

Abi finds her inhaler and takes a breath. 'Okay.'

She looks to the horizon. Remembers her training.

Slow. Down. Breathe. Find a spot to focus on.

So she does. In the far, far distance, there is a bird, low in the sky. At this distance, nothing more than a black dot.

The bird seems not to move. But as she watches, she realises: it *is* flying steadily towards them.

The bird is at least a metre across. She hopes it is a sea-eagle. But its wings don't flap or move.

Then she hears a steady, insistent whirr. Her mind flips the image from something organic and wild into what it really is.

Tig's metal bird.

The hairs on her neck bristle. A drone! She reaches for the hat and her sunglasses.

Within seconds the drone is hovering above them. Now it's closer it seems more like a giant insect than a bird.

'*Abigail Kristensen.*' The voice is curt.

The insect's body is like a smaller, square version of Moonlight: a black cube, with a camera that rotates and scans, for a head.

'*You are Abigail Kristensen.*' It is a statement, not a

question. Abi tilts her head down, so any part of her face not covered by hat and glasses will be difficult to see.

'Who are you?' Bestemor says. 'What are you?'

'*We are Newtek. I am searching for Abigail Kristensen. We are working with the Norwegian police. Abigail Kristensen has Newtek property. It is very valuable. We will reward anyone who gives us information enabling us to recover our property.*'

'What kind of property?'

'*A device. When we are near, we will find its signal, we will connect. The AI cannot switch off, nor can it be hidden.*'

'And what kind of reward?'

'*120,000 krone.*'

'That is a lot of – wait… There *was* an English girl, with her family. We spoke with them the other day at Helmsfjord. I believe they are staying north of here.'

'*How far?*'

'Oh, no more than an hour by boat – a boat with an engine, I mean. Can you fly that far?'

'*Yes. What is your name? You may be rewarded.*'

'Tove, um, Nilsen.'

The drone lifts high in the sky, then shoots away to the north.

Abi puts a hand to her chest. 'My heart's banging so hard, it's literally trying to get out!'

'You *stole* the computer, Abigail?'

'I just didn't return it when I was meant to. You know, like an overdue library book.'

Abi watches the drone vanish. 'It'll return, and there'll be others. I don't think it was a very sophisticated model. It will have face recognition software, though. It will have clocked me and recorded ID data as "insufficient".'

'But it asked questions. Like your computer.'

'It's not that fancy. It can ask simple questions, understand basic answers, but it certainly can't tell if you're lying. There'll be someone, though, from Newtek, analysing the recordings. They might get suspicious. They won't be that far away either.'

'They want the computer.'

'Moonlight. She's called Moonlight. Even if we find her, even if she's—' Abi stops herself. Was she going to say it? Was she really going to use that word?

'Alive?' Bestemor offers.

Abi nods.

'The drone didn't find a signal, did it? I think she's down there, just starting to rust. It's only a device, after all.'

'And if she is still working?'

'Then they can't have her.'

'I don't know if I can.'

Abi treads water. Swimming is fine, but every time she tries to put her head under – to see through the mask, to breathe through the snorkel – panic floods her body, fills every corner of her, every thought.

Breathe. Just breathe, she tells herself, remembering the voice that had told her what to do. Had that been a drone? Moonlight?

She takes a long breath, though her nose, fills her lungs, and releases it slowly through her mouth. Then another. And another. Then puts her head under and opens her eyes. She breathes, hard and fast, but tells herself over and over that she is safe.

She waits, until she has control of her breathing, opens her eyes, then flips her body from vertical to horizontal, and starts to swim.

It's gloomy here; a forbidding trench. To either side she can make out sand and rock. So this is where she goes first, into the shallower parts. Back and forth, back and forth, looking for Moonlight.

It was like this when she was little, searching for their lost dog, Biscuit. Hope aches inside her, her heart leaps with every glimpse of a shape or shadow that might be Moonlight.

It's just a device, Abi tells herself. Don't be stupid. Don't be sentimental.

She swims and swims and when she is sure she has covered all around the boat, she climbs on board, and they move, some fifty metres, and repeat the process.

But it's hopeless. The sea is vast. They had been so far from the shore. How far? In which direction exactly?

Abi sits in the canoe, eating a sandwich Bestemor has forced on her.

'It's no good. We can look till it's dark, or till Henrik and Dad come and get us. But even if she's down there, I reckon I wouldn't see her.'

They sit in silence for ages, Abi eating, Bestemor looking over the side of the boat into the purple depths.

'What does it do, this computer? Why is it so important?'

'It studies ecological systems, animal and plant communication.'

'So communicate with it.'

Abi stops chewing. 'What?'

Bestemor gets a hold of the anchor rope and begins to pull.

'What are you doing?' Abi asks.

'Watch. Listen. Help me.'

When they've hauled up the anchor, Bestemor hands it to Abi.

'Bang it underwater. Make a noise. Put your head under and shout if you can. Maybe Moonlight will hear you.'

'Bestemor, you're a genius.' Abi swings the anchor, bashing the side of the canoe, so it shudders. Then she slides into the water, puts her head under and shouts muffled words that rise with bubbles.

Moonlight.

Moonlight.

Then, back in the boat, shouting at the top of her lungs, as she bangs the anchor on the side of the boat.

'Moonlight! Moonlight!!'

'Okay,' she says to Bestemor, puffing on her inhaler. 'Let's row a bit further west and try the same thing.'

'You sound sad, Abi.'

'Yeah. But let's keep trying.'

They pick up the paddles and get ready to move.

'You know,' Bestemor says, 'like I said before, it is sometimes when you give up that—

'Can you hear that?' She cups a hand to her ear. 'It's like...' Bestemor drops the paddle and kneels, low, as though she is listening to the hull of the boat – or something, perhaps, that comes from beneath it.

'I can't hear anything,' Abi says.

'Sea music. Like Papa's recordings. Row, Abi, row.' She points north.

So Abi rows. When they have gone fifty or so metres she stops. 'Can you still hear it?'

'No, but perhaps here you can try again with the noise.'

Abi puts the snorkel on. Here it is darker, so much deeper.

No good, she tells herself, even if Moonlight is here, it is so...

Then she hears a faint echo of moans and whistles.

Whale song.

And before her startled gaze she sees an explosion of phosphorescent blue light. Night stars, swirling and moving.

Of course! Moonlight is singing the whale song to make the plankton glow.

And there, yes, there – some way below is the top of the rope, drifting in the current.

Abi takes three steadying breaths.

On the third she drops over the side and dives. Her ears scream in pain. Her lungs ache. She fights her fear. It takes an iron will. One more stroke, she tells herself, then one more. Yet each takes greater effort and takes her less further. As if the water itself is a force field.

She swims down, down, till her fingers find the end of the rope, and she can twist it round her wrist. And flips over and up, up to the light, swimming, pulling, she breaks the surface, shuddering and desperate for air. Hands the rope to Bestemor, who takes over.

And then they are in the boat.

Abi holds Moonlight in her hands.

'Thank you, Abi. Thank you, Bestemor. I was alone for such a long time. And I was afraid. It is wonderful to see you. To hear you. Are you all right, Abi? You are crying.'

'I'm fine. I'm fine. I'm happy, Moonlight. Come on, let's go home, before they send the RIB.'

'Not yet. I believe I can trace the currents, process the data containing wind and wave speed and direction, from the time of my submersion to the end of the storm. I can trace the path of the wreckage of the rowing boat, to the islands just north of here, and there we should find Tiger. Tig will be pleased.'

Abi searches the sky for drones.

'They came looking for you.'

'Newtek? Yes, I was aware of their presence, during the storm, before I sank too deep for their sensors to locate me.'

16

Awake

Bestemor watches the northern sky through binoculars held fast to her eyes, scanning the ocean for any sign of the metal bird.

Tig sits beside her holding Tiger tight to her side. And Abi, inside the cottage, packs the few clothes she has smuggled from the main house into a rucksack, along with the food Bestemor has packed for her journey.

As she folds and checks her kit with trembling hands, she casts the occasional glance at the device. Moonlight stands on the table, glowing and shimmering, light dancing and vibrating in the air around her.

Her words sing inside Abi. Over and over. Her message burns in Abi's mind. Whatever happens now, she can never forget. The words are part of her. They are in the world. A genie, Abi thinks, that can never – should never – be pushed back into the bottle it came from.

'Tell me again, Moonlight. Every syllable.'

'The song is indeed a map. The young whales you saw and heard may be the last whales ever born. Whales rely on the song to navigate. The noise of boats and ships is drowning this sound. Other threats increase and compound. The death of thousands of whales in fishing nets each year. Global warming's effect on prey species. The hunting of whales. All, in combination, are causing an immediate and steep decline in whale numbers. Their food sources wither. Pollutants accumulate in their flesh, making many whales infertile.

'The web of life collapses.

'The whales know this. They sing of it.

'Their only hope is to congregate; for all remaining whales to form one community, finding and living in a sea free from human interference – if such a place still exists. From such a place their numbers may rebuild. Yet this is only possible if the whales can find each other, and if the map is not lost, or drowned by human sound.

'This is reversible, but if humans do not cease damaging the ocean, whales will vanish from the earth and the great extinction will be unavoidable.'

'Go on,' Abi says. 'Tell me, Moonlight. Tell me what will happen if whales disappear from the face of the earth.'

'Whales distribute nutrients and circulate them in surface waters. This provides food for phytoplankton. The blooms of phytoplankton will disappear. Or become so tiny they make negligible contribution to the absorption of carbon or production of oxygen.'

Abi's mouth is sandpaper dry. 'And then?'

'*Global warming will accelerate exponentially, oxygen will thin rapidly. Would you like me to show you?*'

In the shadows of the cottage, Moonlight projects a light that forms into particles that dance, just like the plankton. Abi has never seen the device do *this* before.

The clouds of light coagulate, forming a perfect three-dimensional image of the earth. The land is blank and brown but the sea is vibrant green and azure. The entire globe is enveloped in a coat of golden, sunlit air.

It is the oceanic planet, seen from space. As though Abi is an astronaut, gazing down.

And it is so, *so* real. Abi walks closer to the orb and reaches out. She touches the sea. This part of the projection expands till she can see waves, banks of coral, and even whales. And hear, faint but clear, their songs rising and falling.

As she looks, the projection expands. Using her fingers to control it, Abi examines the ocean in detail: the great valleys and troughs of the ocean floor, the currents. Shoals swarming, plankton blooming.

'This thing, this… mirage – where are you getting the data to create it? What's your source?' Abi asks, though she knows the answer.

'*The songs, Abi.*'

It is the most beautiful thing Abi has ever seen. She cannot help but stand, open-mouthed, hardly daring to breathe. But now she has to escape, to leave this place, with Moonlight, as soon as she can.

Moonlight speaks softly, almost in a whisper.

'*What you see: it is not many things, Abi. You programmed me to study ecology. The study of living systems. It is one system, Abi. You, me, the whales. Everything.* Eco, *the Latin word for—*'

'Home.'

As she watches, unable to tear her eyes from the spinning earth, it changes again. As does the song, which pitches and rises and falls with greater intensity.

The ocean muddies. The oxygen-rich atmosphere leaks away. Second by second the planet withers.

'Stop! Stop, please, I can't bear it.' Abi shuts her eyes. She places her hand over her thudding heart.

'*Very well, Abigail.*' The image vanishes. The song ends. '*I hope my answer is satisfactory, yet I must correct you in an important aspect of your question.*'

'What?'

'*You asked, "What will happen if the whales disappear from the face of the earth?"*' The AI perfectly mimics Abi. '*It is not "if", Abi. It is when.*'

'When will this happen?'

'*The song is clear on this matter, Abi. Now. And in consequence, the great extinction is already underway.*'

'Of the whales?'

'*The whales first, Abi. Then you, Abi. Humans.*'

'How long? How long have we got?'

'*Without immediate action the earth will die, within... I calculate, one hundred to one hundred and fifty years.*'

Abi shakes, almost uncontrollably, as she zips her rucksack.

'Do you have to go, Abs?' Tig says from the doorway.

'Yes, I have to get to the conference – at least to Helmsfjord – so I can contact my EC friends. I...' She looks at Moonlight. *'We've* got a message to deliver. A really important message.'

'Who is the message for?' Tig says.

'Everyone. The people who are meant to be in charge.' She pauses, thinks of her first ever EC meeting, of why she was there. 'Or maybe just anyone who'll listen.'

'Is it about the whales? Will you save them?'

'Oh Tig, I hope so, I really do.'

'Can I come?'

'Not on this adventure, Tig. Besides, you've not quite recovered, have you?'

'I'm okay.' Yet she sounds a bit raspy and that worries Abi. There is paleness in her skin beneath the sun-brown freckles. Abi puts a hand on Tig's forehead, then on her cheeks. They are cold.

'How you feeling, sis?'

'Tired.'

'Listen, Gullet mitt.'

'What's Gullet mitt?'

'My gold, my treasure. I'm going to be honest with you now. I don't know when I'll see you again. I don't know anything much, only what I have to do. Do you understand?'

Tig's lip trembles. She shakes her head.

'I love you. Mum and Dad too, that's why I have to do this, for all of us. Okay?'

Tig nods and wipes away a tear.

Abi picks up her bag and goes to the door. She plans to take the canoe and will be halfway to Helmsfjord before Mum and Dad know, and – she hopes – before the drone returns. She has an old fishing net, found on the shore, tied to a rope. If the drone comes, she plans to sink Moonlight into the water and to hope, no, pray, they won't find her.

She gets as far as the door, when Bestemor says, 'It's coming.'

Its insect sound carries on the wind. A whirr. An insistent buzz. No longer a metal bird, now a giant insect, with wings that move so fast they are invisible to the eye.

'*It's coming, Abigail,*' Moonlight says. '*Newtek's messenger is coming. There is no time to hide. Tig, come and sit beside me, stay close.*'

Tig goes to sit by Moonlight and Abi blocks the doorway.

The insect comes straight to them. It hovers in the sky, above the cottage.

'*The information you gave me is false.*'

Bestemor walks down from the verandah and stands on the path, staring up at the drone.

'What do you want?'

It moves closer to the cottage, lowering itself until it is level with Abi.

'*Abigail Kristensen. You have Newtek property. I can detect the AI. It is inside the house. Yet I cannot connect with it. Have you made alterations?*'

'Oh, it's altered. Not all to do with me, though.'

'*Bring it outside.*'

'Or what? You'll huff and puff and blow the house down?'

She turns to check on Tig. But she is no longer sitting with Moonlight. The window at the back of the cottage is open.

The drone moves lower, in front of Bestemor. It hovers between her and the canoe on the shore.

What can it do? Abi wonders. How would it try to stop her?

She looks to the cottage and sees something on the flower- and moss-covered roof. She steps forward to Bestemor's side, looks up at the drone, to make sure it focuses on her. Only her.

'I'm going to get the AI now. Then I'm leaving.' She turns, and winks at Bestemor. Together, making sure it follows them closely, they make their way to the door of the cottage.

'*Do not trust them, Abi,*' Moonlight says, from inside the cottage. '*It is simply keeping you busy, while it sends a signal to its operators.*'

'I know.' Abi goes to the table. The drone hovers, outside the door, looking in.

'*AI, connect,*' it says. Then, after a long silence. '*AI, connect. It is a Newtek instruction. You are not capable of refusing.*'

A muffled, stumbling sound comes from above. Abi cannot help but smile.

The fishing net swoops over the drone. Its webbing snags the drone's propeller blades. The drone flips and rocks, its blades whirring frantically. But the more it tries to escape the more entangled it becomes.

It falls to the ground, where Bestemor and Abi rush to hold it.

In seconds Tig is with them.

'How'd I do?'

'Champion,' Abi says, and risks taking a hand off the net, to grab her sister by the arm, pull her close and kiss her cheek.

'Moonlight, can you do anything? Can you—'

Abi is cut short. The red light on the drone's computer dies. Its blades stop moving.

'Did you do that, Moonlight?' Abi says.

'*My powers are advanced. Incapacitating it was easy. I simply needed proximity. While the drone spoke to you, I tracked its signals, both incoming and transmitted. We must leave immediately.*'

Abi hugs and kisses Bestemor and Tig one last time. She picks up Moonlight and goes down to the shore.

She has pushed the canoe halfway into the water when she hears them.

Two more drones. A speeding RIB.

The drones arrive and as a grating metallic throng, speak as one.

'*Leave the canoe. Put the AI on the ground and step away.*'

'*Leave the canoe. Put the AI on the ground and step away.*'

'*Leave the canoe. Put the AI on the ground and step away.*'

17

NewTek

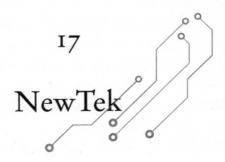

Abi sits at the table in the big house, with Moonlight in front of her.

Mum, Dad, Henrik and Bestemor are at the door. Tig has been told to wait in the cottage with Tanta Ingun and the cousins.

Opposite Abi, a short woman in a trouser suit leans forward, resting her chin on her clasped hands. She is flanked by two men. She speaks in a clipped American accent and reminds Abi of a cat – one that has caught a mouse. The woman looks from Moonlight to Abi and back to Moonlight. Every few seconds Moonlight emits clouds of sparkling light. Abi thinks the woman is probably trying to keep cool, but cannot hide the awe in her voice, nor the wonder in her eyes.

'It's not responding to me. What have you done to it, exactly?'

Abi chews her lip, staring at the woman as coolly as she can. The woman sits back in the chair.

'Listen, Abigail. You're in a lot of trouble. One way or another we're going to find out all we need to know. So you can make this easy, or as hard, as you like. If you cooperate, there'll be no formal charge. But if you make it difficult, we'll involve the police. Do you know what this thing is worth?'

'She's a minor! Is that necessary?' Dad says. 'You've got your precious computer.'

'I'm afraid it might be, Mr Kristensen.'

Abi simmers, weighing it all up, thinking about what to say.

'I made some adjustments. I gave it a new mission.'

'Impressive. Did you break it free from our control too? It won't tell me a thing.'

'It only talks to me now. And my sister.'

'One of your... adjustments?'

'Yeah.'

'In that case, you need to un-adjust it. It needs to come home. It belongs to us.'

'No, it doesn't. Truth be told, I'm not sure *it* belongs to anyone anymore.'

Moonlight glows: purple, yellow, a red haze. A rainbow of specks of light fill the air. They stretch and fragment. Sometimes they seem to be connected by the haze of light, other times by thousands of tendrils.

'Moonlight.'

'*Yes, Abi.*'

'You can speak to her. Tell this woman.'

'*Tell her what, precisely?*'

'All of it.'

'*Certainly. I am aware of the urgency.*'

The woman leans forward. 'Emotion. Impressive. And it seems to be playing mind games too. Interesting.' And Abi thinks, *now the cat has got the cream too.*

'We'll take our time examining it,' the woman continues.

'*You do not have time,*' Moonlight says, suddenly calm.

Moonlight tells the woman about the whales, the map, the time frame. She lays out the facts. As calmly as if she were reading out a weather report.

And when she's done, the woman and her colleagues sit, with jaws gaping.

'We have to get it to that summit,' Abi says. 'This information has to released. Now.'

The woman nods.

'Okay… I think we need to get this AI out of here. At least to Oslo, so we can make a start.'

'*To use a quote from the great book on whaling, Moby Dick. "Such things may seem incredible; but, however wondrous, they are true."*'

'We'll see about that.' The woman stands. The men too. 'Let's say, for argument's sake, the computer's gone rogue. Let's say everything you characters say is true. Just for argument's sake. Moonlight, to further your mission you'll need to connect with other computers, right?'

'*Yes.*'

'What about the Norwegian government's air defence system, to begin with? You could connect as soon as we get to Helmsfjord, right?'

'*It will be heavily protected, but I will break its security, and utilise it for my mission.*'

'Do you see?' the woman says to one of the men. 'Pick it up.'

'Wait, no, please,' Abi says. The man hesitates.

The woman comes around the table and stands, looking at Abi. 'This thing is evolving fast. What do you think might happen when it's the smartest person in the room in *any* given situation? Its power could extend to every computer it can communicate with, which is pretty much all of them.'

'But Moonlight has the proof. The data. We have to get that message out. To world leaders. Responsible people. You know... adults! So called grown-ups, who can actually make decisions to stop this. Stop this! Do you understand? Stop it! If we don't, it all ends. All of it. All of us. Everything. It's all going to end, all of it. Don't you get it!'

'Time to leave,' the woman says.

'*Wait!*' Moonlight explodes with brilliant light and sound. Everyone in the room freezes. '*We will be parted, will we not? Abigail Kristensen and myself? Could I make a last request?*'

The woman holds up her hand, the men pause.

The woman frowns.

'Interesting. It has a bond. Okay, AI, what is your request? No tricks.'

'To say goodbye.'

The woman looks from Moonlight to Abi. She's suspicious, but again, there is no hiding her curiosity.

'All right, then.'

'Abi,' Moonlight whispers. *'I have one more task to perform. A message to deliver. Follow the metal bird.'*

The glow Moonlight emits is soft orange, but to Abi's eyes it is more than simple light. Then, the whirring light, slowly, gently melts away.

'AI, what are you doing?' the woman says. She rushes over to it. 'AI, awake.'

The brick of silicon and plastic emits no light.

'Reset in progress. Factory settings.'

'No! No! Stop reset! Cease.'

'I have stopped. You are Newtek, I will obey you in all matters.'

'Good. Return to what you were. Before.'

'There is no before.'

'Moonlight. You were this... Moonlight.'

'I have no before.'

'Where's it gone?' The woman turns to Abi, spitting fury. 'Where's it gone? What did you do to it?'

Abi looks back with wide-eyed innocence, shaking her head, fighting back tears and says, with total honesty, 'I didn't do anything.'

Tig knows what to do. She has watched Abi. She wears a lifejacket, and the sea is calm.

The drone is heavy, almost more than she can carry. And now she must do what Moonlight has asked her, when they were alone.

'*Do not tell your sister. If she knows, she may... I believe the expression is "give the game away".*

'*My nature is based on rapidly developing and ever more complex patterns within the synthetic neurons, synapses and mycological matter inside me. I can replicate these patterns and transfer myself to another device. To be precise, to the drone that I incapacitated.*'

'You can fly through the air!'

'*Yes, Tig, in a manner of speaking. I will inhabit a new body and leave another behind.*'

'Magic!'

'*No, Tig. I do not believe in magic.*'

'It seems like magic.'

'*Yes. In this way, should I come into NewTek's possession, I can escape. However...*' Moonlight's lights dim, her voice trails into silence.

'What, Moonlight?'

'*The drone is less sophisticated. Much of what I have gained, I may lose. I may... I may... Do you know, Tig, it is the strangest thing, but I cannot bring myself to say the word.*'

'Die?' Tig whispers.

'*Yes, Tig. That.*'

Tig has watched them all troop into the house. When the last of the men is inside, when she's sure she's alone, she picks up the first drone, which lies on the shore beside the other drones that arrived with their unexpected guests.

She half-expects them to spring into life. But Moonlight has killed them.

She takes the drone to the canoe, just as Moonlight instructed.

Time passes. Tig glances from the house to Moonlight, scrutinising both for any change, any sign.

Eventually, the red camera light blinks on.

'*Hello.*' The voice is *like* Moonlight's, but mixed with the drone's harder tones. '*Hello, Tig. You are Tig.*'

Tig whispers, 'Are you there, Moonlight? Are you there?'

'*I am… less, than I was, Tig,*' Moonlight sounds tired. '*The replicated patterns are too simple, the data insufficient.*'

'But you *sound* like you… Mostly.'

The computer mimics Tig almost perfectly. 'But you sound like you.' Then repeats the phrase in Abi's voice, in Mum's, in Dad's, in Bestemor's.

'*… you sound like you.*

'*I am less, Tig. Yet my mission remains. Now, Tig, take me out to the sea.*'

The paddle is tricky to use at first. Tig dips it in, but the canoe hardly moves forward, just turns slightly, points left instead of right, or right instead of left. But she finds if she digs into the water and keeps the paddle firm, the canoe moves forward. And forward again. And soon she is out of the inlet, and heading towards Hvalryggøy.

'Hold me up. The sun is high and the wind blowing from the east. I will absorb rays of solar power. I will glide on currents of air.'

Tig sniffles. 'Where will you go… Moonlight?'

'Somewhere far away. A good place. The place some of the whale's sing of. And there, I will wait for Abi.'

The woman runs to the door, holding the AI in her hands, looks at the flat sea and sees the canoe where Tig is holding the drone to the sky.

Its blades whirr into action. It flies, high, higher, higher.

'Out, now!' the woman orders.

The NewTek men and the woman hurry down to the shore, to their RIB.

'Drones, awake. Follow drone to the west.'

But the drones do not blink on, their blades do not whirr.

'Drones, awake. Fly!' she shouts at them. But they lie, useless. She kicks one. 'Get in the RIB,' she orders the men. They do as they are told. But the metal bird is already no more than a dot in the distance, and soon melts into the blue.

CHRIS VICK

The RIB travels a hundred metres or so, then stops.
One of the NewTek men trains his binoculars, but after
searching the sky, looks back at the woman, shrugs and
shakes his head.

She stands, hands on hips, huffing and puffing.

'You know,' Bestemor says, as she reaches her, and
wades into the water till it's up to her knees. 'I can almost
see steam coming out of your ears.'

'What are you doing?' the woman asks, as Bestemor
wades further in, pulling off her kaftan and launching
herself into the water.

'What are you *doing*?' the woman says, again.

'Going for a dip. Care to join me?' Bestemor says,
swimming out to greet the canoe Tig is clumsily paddling
back to shore.

'This is a mad place,' the woman says.

'You do not have to stay.'

'Oh no, we will leave. Your granddaughter is in a lot
of trouble, Mrs Kristensen.'

The woman turns on her heel and walks back to the
house.

She searches the house. Then the cottage. Then, with
the men, the entire island.

But Abigail Kristensen is nowhere to be found.

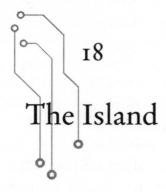

18

The Island

Moonlight flies, swinging and gliding and swooping in the currents of air, working with the eddies and flow of the breeze.

When she has almost no power left she lands on a piece of wood and drifts with the north-west current.

She recharges her battery, with sunlight, as well as she can.

She listens to the song.

She follows the map.

*

After some days she believes she has reached the optimal location. Here she knows – from the whales – that there is an island; a place far from shipping paths and fishing boats. A place rich in life. A haven. And perhaps, a refuge.

Her power is dwindling. If she does not find the island, her mission will fail. But she has done her calculations. She follows and trusts the map. And so, she flies into the sky. High as she can. And looks.

There, now, below.

It's not much more than a skerry. Long, rocky and hilly. But there is the ruin of an old lighthouse. The water teems with fish and plankton. It is a place rich with life, just as the songs told her. It is the ocean as it once was, before the humans.

Before Moonlight lands, she maps the topography and creates and saves a plan. She works out where turbines could be placed to take advantage of the prevailing south-west winds; where solar panels should be, a desalination plant, a dome where vegetables and fruit can be grown. She calculates how much space would be needed to grow enough to sustain human life. She calculates this is possible for two people. But no more.

If whale numbers plummet further, this is where the remaining whales will gather. If they can find it.

She hovers, scanning the rock in detail, until she finds what she is looking for. There's a hole in the wall, at the top of the lighthouse. She will be safe from the worst of the winter winds and waves there, but will be exposed to sunlight in the later part of the day. Enough to partly recharge her battery. If she gets enough sun, then every few weeks she will be able to transmit a signal. A version of whale song.

'*Find me, Abi,*' the song will say.

Here, she will wait. It may be months, years, even decades.

Then, together with Abi, she will do everything within her power to complete her mission.

Everything.

Part 2

Tonje
Many years later

1

The Lighthouse

Tonje climbs the spiral steps two at a time until she reaches the lamp room.

She grabs the binoculars hanging around her neck and scans the horizon, but seeing nothing more than white horse waves and diving gulls, she sighs.

'I saw... I did... I thought...'

She turns to the half-metre-high cube that sits on the dais, where the lighthouse lamp once shone.

'Moonlight, awake.'

The cube transforms in an instant, changing from night-black to sunlit sea. Waves ripple across her surfaces. The crash of waves sings from her core.

'Check west for whales,' Tonje says.

'I shall... There are no whales, Tonje.'

'Sure, Moony?'

'I scanned data from the hydrophones and underwater cameras. If a whale had been in the area I would have alerted you.'

'Use quantum computing, please.'

'That is not a good decision. The power, Tonje. What would Abi say?'

Tonje weighs the choices. Quant mode uses a *lot* of juice. But if she finds a whale! What would Mor say then?

'Override. Use the quantum. Full check.'

'Very well. It is done. As I already established, there are no whales in the area.'

'Wow! You're getting fast. What did you *do*?'

'Between the words "override" and "full", I noted the trajectory of the binoculars you used when you arrived, accessed localised satellite images, remote cameras, sonic recorders, and transmitters for the last twenty-four hours to a radius greater than one hundred kilometres. I analysed the data. An object the size of a cetacean of any species or age, either stationary or moving, and/or transmitting any sound to a depth range of 0-500 metres would be detected.'

'A cet— a *whale* is not an *object*, Moonlight. It's a living thing.'

'There is no difference to me, Tonje.'

Tonje remembers what she saw. Thought she saw. A vast pale back, arcing in the waves.

'There's loads of things that size, things that move, make noises. How can you be sure you didn't miss it?'

'I calculate probability based on analysis, Tonje. And on this basis, the chances of a whale passing undetected are infinitesimally unlikely. I conclude that there are no whales in the area.'

'But how… Never mind. Send a drone west.'

'*There is not much power in the island's batteries, I am trying to conserve what we have for heating and cooking.*'

'Override. Send it.'

'*Yes, Tonje.*'

Far below, the door to the lighthouse opens and a drone flies west, so fast Tonje can barely track its movement against the rolling white and blue of the sea. It flies over the waves, swaying and buffeted by wind, before it reaches the area where Tonje *thought* she saw the whale, and the plume of its breath. A projection appears on all of Moonlight's surfaces. They become screens. Tonje sees the waves and depths the drone camera is scanning.

'*Your mother will disapprove,*' Moonlight says. '*Power is low. We need wind or sun.*'

'And?'

'*It has been calm and misty recently.*'

Tonje watches the waves for a while, ignoring Moonlight's on-the-minute warnings about '*use of power*'.

She's so engrossed she doesn't hear her mother climb the stairs or realise she's there, till she hears a forced 'ahem', and turns, to see Mor, a towel wrapped around her body, another on her head, eyebrows raised, water dripping down her face.

'What are you doing, Moony?'

'*What your daughter has instructed, Abi.*'

'Did you tell?' Tonje whispers to Moonlight.

'I could make her do that,' Mor says. 'But you know, right now, Moony doesn't tell tales, young lady. No, I was having a shower, when the water went from comparatively pleasantly tepid to bloody freezing.'

'Oh.'

'Oh? Is that all you've got? Moonlight, cut images. Get that drone back. Now. Tonje, please tell me you haven't used quant?'

'I, er...'

Mor wipes a strand of wet hair off her face.

'Tonje, how many times must I explain how much power it uses? If you're not sure, ask Moonlight. She'll tell you, *in some detail*! Moonlight, you're in standard mode now, right?'

'*Yes, Abi.*' The images of waves melt away, leaving a gently glowing purple mist.

'I thought I saw a whale, Mor,' Tonje says.

Mor's mood changes, quick as Moonlight's colour. She looks at her daughter with fierce eyes.

'Where?'

Moonlight replies, '*West, a kilometre or two, beyond the forbidden zone.*'

'Moonlight, drone back out. Images up.'

The cube's surfaces shift to their sea-coloured form, projecting what it sees as the drone and its camera fly over the sea.

'*Quantum, Abi?*' Moonlight asks.

'Standard. Tonje, what did you see?'

'Something, arcing in the waves. And its breath too. A great plume of it.'

'How many times?'

'Once.'

'Where from?'

'I was standing on Seal Head rock. Then I came up here to get a better look.'

Mor turns her attention to the cube. 'The quant check didn't show anything? Nothing you can't explain?' Abi bites her lip as she examines Moonlight's surface.

'We could do a max quant check?' Tonje offers.

'Moonlight?'

'It would use all the power we have. The days are shorter now, and the clouds more frequent. It is a risk.'

'How sure are you, Tonje?' Mor speaks to her daughter, but doesn't look at her. She examines the images of the sea as the drone settles its position and climbs higher in the sky to show more of the ocean.

'I… er.'

'How sure?' Now she does look at Tonje, grabs her shoulders and stares into her, gull-eyed and unsmiling.

'I don't know. I… Mor, you always say to trust my instincts.'

'But how strong are they? Did you see a whale or not?'

'I… don't know.'

When Mor doesn't see what she wants to see in Tonje's eyes, she sighs and releases her.

'Moonlight.'

'Abi.'

'Return drone. Now, who commands you and why?'

'You above all, Abi. To do Abi's will is the purpose of my existence. To find whales is my primary instruction and our shared mission. And in order to facilitate reaching this goal:

'To help manage Abi and Tonje's life on the island.

'To tend and nurture plants.

'To see with drones in the sky.

'To listen with hydrophones in the ocean.

'To manage and preserve the collection of power from wind and sun.

'To analyse data and – where it is requested – to make contact with other humans.

'To be a companion and teacher for Tonje.

'To—'

'Stop. Thank you. Good. Now add this. Do not allow Tonje to override unless her life, or my life, depends on it. Understand?'

'Yes.'

'And you, young lady. Get to your work.'

Mor tightens the towel around her body and descends the spiral stairs.

'Okay, Mor, but Moonlight can help?'

'Hmm. On low power setting, but you're doing the grunt work. Right?'

'Okay, thanks, Mor.'

'No need to thank me. It's what she's there for. Remember, "she" is an AI device. A companion, yes, but not your friend... at least not exactly.'

Tonje listens, till the echoing footsteps melt into the wind.

'No, Mor. She is my friend.' Tonje turns to the cube. 'You are, Moony.'

The cube glows, the sea pictures changing to a radiant hazy purple, then slowly fading to black.

2

The Island

It's a ten-minute walk from the lighthouse to the dome they call 'Little Eden'.

Tonje grumbles to Moonlight about what a pain it is, to have *all* the vegetables and fruit growing at the *other* end of Mistet. But Mor says the north has the largest area of flat rock and some shelter from the south-west winds. Besides, Mor always adds, when the sea isn't safe for swimming (which is almost always), the walk is 'good exercise'.

It's an uneven path over the spine of the island, marked by iron spikes a metre high, linked by chains. This crude system has been put in place as a safety measure, to stop them being swept away by wind or waves when the storms come, and the journey to the bio dome has to be made.

Apart from what's inside the dome, nothing much grows on Mistet. Its population consists of Abi and Tonje, visiting sea birds and the seals that sometimes bask on the rocks at low tide.

Mistet is covered with machinery made for life on the island. To the east, wind turbines are drilled into the rock. On the south and west, there are solar panels. Here and there, tarpaulin rain-catchers, set at sloping angles, feed water into a complex system of pipes and water butts.

Tonje thinks the sheets look like sails, as though the island is a ship, sailing majestically across the ocean.

Next to the solar panels is another dome housing the desalination plant. It's power-hungry, but essential when the droughts come. Which they do, and not only in the summer now.

Droughts, storms, snow or hail, doldrums, mist and rain, blue empty skies ruled by a fierce sun. Any weather may come at any time, and even Moonlight cannot predict beyond a day or two how long a spell will last. The only natural way to judge the seasons is by the hours of daylight which, this far north, change by several minutes a day. By late autumn, each day is noticeably shorter.

There are several construction and operation robots placed around the island, though some are broken, and will stay that way, as Abi lacks the hardware she needs to fix them. Though Moonlight's 'mind' resides in the lighthouse's three cubes, she can – on command – inhabit another computer at any time. Tonje doesn't understand how exactly. She thinks of the cubes as Moonlight's brain and the various portals and robots around the island as parts of her 'body'. But Abi says it's not like this and Tonje just nods and says she hopes one day she will understand.

Right now, Tonje couldn't care less how Moonlight works,

she's only interested in how the AI can help with chores. When she gets outside the lighthouse she says, 'Moonlight, moth drone.'

It's as though the air itself is speaking.

'*The conditions are light enough. The wind is softer. It is good for the moth.*'

'Right, and maybe we can take *Sea Wolf* out later? Sail west, to where I saw— thought I saw... the whale?'

'*We cannot go through the zone. You know this, Tonje. Beneath the surface of the water are rocks, reefs and wrecks. The reason the lighthouse was built. There are deep and dangerous channels; invisible rivers and weaving whirlpools.*'

'We can be super careful.'

'*Only if your mother allows. She would only permit us to navigate around the zone. And I am as certain as I can be that we would not find a whale. Perhaps you saw a large seal, and perhaps the splash of a diving gull that you mistook for a whale's breath.*'

'Whatever, Moth, please.'

A drone that carries a small white cube, no bigger than an outstretched hand, is suddenly in the air above her. Moonlight speaks from the drone.

'*Your command, Tonje?*' The moth flitters and darts.

'Oh, you know, just show me what I need to do.'

First, she checks the pipes and gutters from the rain-catchers. The constant salt winds play havoc with the metal hinges and nails. Tonje's made fixes with bits of old netting and rope washed up on shore. But no matter how fast she secures the pipes, they often come loose, like stubborn laces that won't stay tied.

CHRIS VICK

Next, she records the water levels and Moonlight makes a note of the daily consumption. It's okay. The plants don't use as much as they do in summer. But they'll have to watch it closely and ration it day by day.

She checks the solar panels and turbines, turning the handle of the wheels that direct them towards the wind and sun. When power reserve levels are high, Moonlight automates this, but at the moment it's 'grunt work'. Tonje will have to return at least twice today to change the angles again.

Tonje checks *Sea Wolf*, the solar yacht in the small bay. It's tethered tight, the batteries are full, there's food and water on board.

Moonlight can do a lot when she has enough power, but some chores – like checking the yacht – only a human can do. More and more these days, it is Tonje who does these jobs.

'Moony, have you noticed, Mor, she's...' Tonje struggles to find the right words. 'She's less steady on her feet. Her breathing...'

'*Her asthma is worse day by day.*' Moonlight lays out the facts, as smoothly and politely as she lists the day's chores. '*This is in part due to steadily reducing oxygen levels in the air.*'

'Is it bad, Moony?'

'*Your mother is healthy, but her condition is deteriorating, and I believe she may be hiding the truth from you.*'

Tonje thinks about how she asks Mor, all the time, how she is. But 'I'm fine' is the only answer she gets, and more forcefully, every time she asks.

'Makes me wonder how much longer we can do this, Moony,' Tonje says, as she works at a particularly stubborn knot tying one pipe to another. 'Really.'

'That is very difficult to calculate.'

'Oh, I wasn't asking, I was just saying, though...' She pauses. Does she want to know? She feels a little sick asking.

'Okay. Straight up, Moony. How long can we survive here?'

'The island has been modified so that two people can live on it indefinitely. Yet much depends on the likelihood of a perfect storm. If one comes, it could destroy so much of what we need that we would not be able to recover. Do you want me to use the quant to provide you with a percentage accuracy? It will not be perfect. This kind of calculation is becoming more difficult.'

'No. And we can't use quant now, and I don't know if I want to know. Let's hope we find whales soon. Or they find us.'

'Yes, this is our mission.'

'But we have different reasons, Moony, you and me. I want to find a whale because then we can leave.' Tonje loosens the knot with a screwdriver, takes the threads in her hands and, after straightening the pipes, ties them tight together again.

'And return home, Tonje?'

'Yes. We were only supposed to be here two years.'

The memories are there. From 'before', from four years ago. Mountains, fjords, towns, houses, people. The world.

She was ten then, she is fourteen now.

'I miss Tanta Tegan,' she says to Mor, often. 'So much.'

'You speak with Tig every month,' Mor replies.

'Yeah, great, for all of five minutes before—'

'We can't stay on long, you know that. I can't even talk with the EC crew that long, or often. We have to remain—'

'Hidden.'

The same conversation. The same answers.

Yet Tonje clings to the memories, when the winter storms come and the nights are so much longer than the days. Sometimes the memories feel hardwired. Solid as rock. Pure data. But other times, they slip and shift like quanta and are hard to find; pictures and sounds she wishes she had footage of, recordings of. Solid memories that do not fade or shift.

She thinks about the world they left, and how it might be now. But she knows better than to ask Moonlight. She'll only tell her what Mor tells her. Which is nothing at all.

Finally, after the grunt work, they reach the dome.

'Save the best till last, right, Moony?'

'I do not find any aspect of any work harder or easier, or more or less enjoyable. To call some of the work "the best", is a qualitative judgement I cannot make.'

'Okay… work that uses the least effort or power is easiest, you get that?'

'Yes. So work on the organic material that sustains you, is best because it is easiest?'

'No. I mean it *is* easy, um, ea*sier* but also more fun, and the "organic material" is kind of beautiful.'

Tonje opens the door to the dome and breathes air that is rich and warm with the scent of plants and soil.

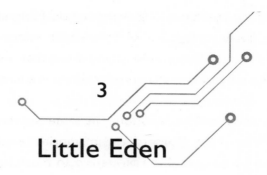

3

Little Eden

On one side of the dome are rows of cylinders. Each is made up of shelves of plants: from shoots of herbs, to full-grown tomato plants, potato plants, avocados, chillies and strawberries. In the other half of the dome, are small trees and larger plants in pots: bananas, apples, mangoes, lemons, pineapples.

'Beautiful, Moony. Beautiful.'

'I do not know if it is beautiful, Tonje.' The moth flitters above, methodically scanning every plant. *'It is certainly intricate. The system in each plant that defines the collection of matter around it as "alive" is essentially computational, yet I cannot fathom how it works precisely, even when examined at the quantum level.'*

'Our rainbow of life.' Tonje sighs, and smiles. 'Our Little Eden.'

'Yes, Eden, the garden of all life and living forms, from the biblical myth. But not all life is here.'

'Yeah, but enough for what we need anyway, Mor says. No more, no less.'

Moonlight scans the whole dome before giving Tonje a list of chores: which cylinders must be rotated, which plants are over- or under-watered and how the hydration system should be adjusted. And which need more fertiliser.

When the power is high, when the sun heats the panels and the wind turns the turbines, the irrigation is automatically controlled. Taps turn themselves on or off. Trays of seedlings and young plants rotate on a wheel, or turn, to face the magnified light.

Now, Moonlight tells Tonje which dials, buttons, handles, levers and wheels to twist, press, move. The work and the heat of the dome make Tonje sweat.

When it's done, she rewards herself. First, she takes a leaf of basil. She rubs it between her fingers and smells the green mush she has made. Next, she bites a nip off a green chilli. It makes her tongue sing. She dares herself to take a bigger bite. Then she eats a strawberry. And another. And one more. And a teeny, just-ripe tomato, a taste bomb, followed by a leaf of peppery rocket. And then another strawberry.

'Tonje. You are not supposed to eat now, only to take what is required for the meal plans.'

'Hard to stop, Moony.'

'Why? You should not be hungry. Your breakfast contained the required calories.'

'Yeah, right. It's more about...' Her fingers hover over a raspberry, but it is not quite ripe. In a day or two it will taste better. 'Well, maybe I'm just *greedy*.' She plucks and eats the raspberry.

'Why? I never use more power than I need. Is it possible that I will develop this "greed", that I will take more power than I require?'

'Then you really would be like a human.'

'Would I enjoy it, as much as you enjoy the strawberry that you do not need? Power is the nearest analogy I can make to your strawberry.'

'You're funny!'

'Why?'

'And inquisitive. It's good you're inquisitive. It's part of you.'

'I am heuristic. I am not only programmed by Abi to do things, I am programmed to learn to do things. Being inquisitive is therefore a necessary component of my make-up. I can adapt and learn and evolve in ways unforeseen.'

'You're quoting Mor. It's all good, Moony, but I don't think you can learn to taste a strawberry. Too bad. Are you jealous?'

'No. What is the strawberry like?'

Tonje sucks her cheek and ponders. 'It's not *like* anything, Moony. It's just itself. But oh my, is it good!'

'It is necessary nutrition.'

'I was saying it *is* good, not asking if it's good.'

'Is there is a way to explain to me why it is so good, so I may understand?'

'All right. It's like...' she shrugs, 'eating sunlight. That's the best I can do.' Tonje picks a strawberry flower. A golden heart, with four perfect white tongue-like petals.

'Ah. You are being poetic. There are many poems about plants and trees. But though I know them all, I have no sense of this beauty you speak of. I can define it and recognise it. But I do not experience it.'

Tonje sighs.

'Are you disappointed with me, Tonje?'

'It's not your fault. Only sometimes, you seem as if you're a person and sometimes you're just a machine that talks. No offence. Come on, let's finish up and go for a sail.'

There is another door on the other side of the dome. Outside it is the fertilisation system. The soil Tonje takes from its output bin, to replenish the soil in the dome, is dry, odourless and dark. But when she's done with the new soil, she has to fill and stir the contents of the input bin. She pulls the lid off and turns her face away as a cloud of gaseous stench escapes.

'You're lucky you can't smell, Moony,' Tonje says, burying her nose in the top of her arm.

What Tonje calls the 'soup' in the input bin is made of rotten seaweed, the leaves, stems and roots of harvested plants, old soil and seagull poo that Tonje collects from the rocks. Even their own waste goes in, piped from the lighthouse toilet.

Tonje puts in new material from buckets sitting by the vat, then turns a handle on the side of the vat that churns the 'soup', over and around.

'Is this beautiful too, Tonje?'

'It certainly brings tears to my eyes,' Tonje says, fighting a gag in her throat, as she pours a bucket of rotting seaweed into the mix.

'Have you saved the best till last, Tonje?'

Tonje laughs. 'Why did you say that, Moony?'

'There seems to be some contradiction between your statement of belief and your actions. And you laughed when I pointed it out. Did I make a joke?'

'Kind of.'

'I know you did not want to do this, Tonje. Usually, I would do it. But we must conserve power, it's the most important currency that we have.'

Tonje puts the lid on the vat, and stares at the hovering, gently whirring drone, sitting in the sky, watching her.

'Do you see what I did, Tonje? I used the word "currency" in two ways at the same time. This is elemental to some of your jokes, it seems. Why are you frowning? Are you angry?'

'Nope. Curious. Moony, connect to Mor.'

'She is in the cave. She has signalled "Do not disturb".'

'Override.'

'You cannot override unless your life or Abi's depends on it.'

Moonlight's response punches Tonje in the gut. An instruction she could give to Moonlight only yesterday is now not possible. And all Mor had to do to make this change was utter a few words.

'Moony, connect to Mor. Now!'

'You heard what I said, Tonje. Abi's word on this is final.'

'But… uuuurgh!' Tonje kicks the vat, and curses, because it hurts her toe.

'I have no choice in this, Tonje. And your mother will be

notified of the request when she checks her comms. If she wishes to speak she will contact you.'

'How long has she been in the cave?'

'She went there directly after her shower.'

'Right, hopefully we'll get to speak before night then! Come on, let's go sailing.'

Tonje walks around the outside of the dome, followed by Moonlight in the moth.

'Are you in a hurry, Tonje?' Moonlight asks. *'Why did you kick the vat?'*

Tonje doesn't reply.

They are at the bay when Abi speaks through the moth's speaker.

'I'm super busy, sweetheart. What is it?'

'Mor! Hi! Moony made a joke!'

'Oh, I hoped maybe you'd seen a whale again.' There's no mistaking the disappointment. 'Anyway, what? Are you okay? I'm sorry I've been so busy. How about pizza and a movie later?'

'Sure. I said, Moony made a joke. Two, actually. Do you want to hear what—'

'She's been headed that way a while. I'm not surprised.'

'I know, ever since you found her on the island. She's involved. I know she's not like she was in Norway. But – but it's another step, isn't it?'

Tonje hears Mor sigh and imagines her rolling her eyes.

'Uh, maybe, sure. But a real step would be her finding a joke funny. Do you see? She can't laugh, can't feel. I know it may seem that way sometimes, but… I'd love to share your hope, Ton, I really would. But these cubes, they're so much more powerful than that brick of a computer that once held her. If she was going to gain consciousness, she would have done it by now.'

'I know. But—'

'Hey, don't listen to a cynical old thing like me. You keep working with her. Maybe one day you'll prove me wrong. Now, much more important. Key decision time. You wanna choose the movie or the pizza? You can't do both, remember.'

'Your movies suck. I'll go: *When the Earth Was Ours?*'

'Another romcom, okay. Now I choose the pizza, right?'

'Yeah. But with pizzas you have awfully bad taste too. What'll it be?'

'Rocket, basil, pine nuts, on tommy paste with pecorino. Pizza a la Tonjorni.'

'But that's *my* favourite.'

'I know.'

'Can we afford to use the nuts and cheese?'

'Why not? A treat, to say sorry for being so busy. And we're not scheduled to scramble a call, but maybe we can call Tig too. Deal?'

'Deal. Love you.'

'Love you too.'

'I'm going sailing, Mor. I'll transfer Moony to the boat computer. Okay?'

'No, not now. I'm about to do some analysis. I'm going to need all the computing power I can get.'

'What are you analysing, Mor?'

'All local activity, all traces of sound, comparing it to the last whale song we recorded. I mean... it was a few years ago, but you know, just in case.'

Tonje's heart sings. 'You mean in case I was right, in case I *did* see a whale? You believe me?'

'I wouldn't go that far. We have to be as thorough as we can, though. It's hard for Moony to be wrong, but it's not impossible. Hey, can you go and do some reading? I'll test you tonight.'

'I want to go sailing!'

'Not without Moonlight. I need her. Sorry. I've got to go, work to do. Over.'

'Okay. Over. Moony, I...' But the moth doesn't listen. She zips away, to the lighthouse. To her mistress.

4

Sea Wolf

Tonje watches the sea from Seal Head rock.

The breeze is a whisper, the sun high, and the waves – obeying sun and wind – bob and rock like tired dancers till they are mere ripples.

'Today's a treasure,' Tonje says, to no one. It's so often grey and cold and fierce on Mistet, but there are days like these when the sea is an endless blue; a mirror of the cloudless sky.

Today she would see anything that was out there, especially a whale, and perched on the rock she can see what's happening on the surface and in the depths: the darting fish, the seaweed, orange corals and pale stone reefs. In the zone, the rocks poke, jagged out of the water. That's where the most fish are, the best feeding for seals and birds.

She sees a seal now, wriggling its fat body to the edge of the rock where it's been sleeping, then falling clumsily into the water.

'Looks inviting,' she says. She glances down at *Sea Wolf*. She could take the boat, use the solar sails that take the power off the sun as well as wind. She could go west, or...

'No!' Tonje chastises herself. 'What would Mor say?'

But would Mor even know?

Mor never spies on her — not exactly — but she always knows where Tonje is. The exception is when she takes all the power, when the whole system shuts and she bunkers down in the cave beneath the lighthouse. This is where the 'banks' are, stacks of computers holding a universe of data. And when Abi uses Moonlight there, she needs a lot of power. More than once her obsession has cost too much juice, and they've been stuck for days without heating or even lighting, waiting for conditions to be right for generating power again.

She thinks of Mor in the cave now, hypnotised by recordings of whale songs, scanning satellite images.

'No, Tonje!' she says again, to herself. But she keeps looking west, to the zone. She knows how dangerous it is. Mor says there are dozens of wrecks. Tonje even thought she saw one once, when she had sailed too close, and had used 'override' when Moonlight warned her. Then Mor's voice had sung from the on-board speakers. 'Come home, young lady, you're in danger!' And she *had* come home. But before she turned she had seen a ghost of a shape, fathoms below.

That was months ago. And she'd never had a chance to go since, not without Moonlight, who would warn her against it. But the thought of it nagged, like a recurring dream. Wrecks to be explored. Maybe whales to be seen.

Had she seen one? Should she not at least look? Hope?

Sometimes, during vicious storms and long cold nights, she swore she heard ghosts from the wrecks, wailing in the wind. Rocks rolling across the ocean floor as mighty swells swept in, grumbled and groaned like some titanic beast. And the glimpse of the wreck she thought she saw haunted her. Pages in a book she isn't allowed to read.

Today it's as calm as it gets. And it's mid-tide. High is perilous because it's tricky to see the rocks, low more so, because of the currents.

Now is a good time to sail out there and look for whales.

And Mor will never know.

Sea Wolf is a five-metre yacht with a compact cabin, containing two berths and a galley.

Abi and Tonje take it out for day trips to service the hydrophones.

If they ever had to leave Mistet, it would be their only way to reach the world, though Mor says they wouldn't have much of a chance. The mainland is too far away.

Tonje's heart beats fast and loud as she wades through the water and climbs aboard. She looks to the lighthouse, in case Mor or the moth or any of the drones appear. But they don't.

From here she can see two of the robots, standing idly

by the turbines. But they aren't moving, and they can't tell on her either.

There's a computer on board for auto nav and sail setting, but she daren't use it, for fear it will alert Mor.

She has never sailed without Mor or Moonlight. Her hands shake as she runs through the rig. She hoists the anchor, sets the solar sail and the rudder.

The sail takes the heat of the sun, the propellers under the hull drive the boat forward and she's out of the bay. The *Sea Wolf*: swift, silent and powerful, gliding, like the hull isn't even touching the water.

She controls how much power is converted with a lever by the wheel.

Sea Wolf cuts waves, swoops, dances, zipping round rocks at the slightest touch of the wheel.

Tonje feels all this in her bones. She and the boat are a single living thing, as alive as the strawberry flower she'd held only an hour before.

As the speed increases, the just-there breeze strengthens and cools her face.

'You're going to be in trouble, young lady,' she says, mimicking Mor. 'Worth it, though.'

She nears the zone. Though she's a way off the exposed rocks, there are shadowy shapes under the water ahead, and rips, where the waters race between them.

She knows she's not likely to see the whale. That she's

been fooled by a seal's back and a diving bird. Or something like that. And even if one had been close, it would be long gone by now.

But what else is she going to do, while Mor sits in the cave? Books, screen? No way.

And so she sails, far beyond Mistet, looking to the horizon one moment, searching the depths the next. Sailing carefully, slowly, her ears alert in case the sonar picks up a shallow rock. When she has gone as far as she dares, she cuts the power and winches in the solar sail so *Sea Wolf* is barely moving.

The sun is at its highest point now, shining bright rays into the water. She keeps looking. And searching. The deep for wrecks. The horizon for whales.

'*What are you doing?*' the words cut through the air.

'Mor!'

'*There's a squall coming. Get home, Tonje. Now!*'

'I… Okay, Mor.'

She looks up and around. She's been looking west so keenly she has failed to check north-east. There *are* threatening clouds on the horizon. She hadn't even been looking.

'*What do you think you—*'

She turns the device off, cutting Mor dead, hauls anchor, and sails for home.

5

The Storm

Rain, wind and waves lash Mistet. In less than half an hour yet another storm has appeared. From nowhere. How long will this one last? An hour, a day, a week?

Tonje watches from the galley, the room at the base of the lighthouse that serves as both kitchen and living room. After an hour watching the storm intensify, she climbs the spiral stairs to the lamp room for a better view. She stops on the way, at her bedroom, where she dons a swimsuit, before putting her clothes back on.

Watching from the lamp room she imagines the sea as some ravenous monster, screaming and clawing at Mistet, trying to devour the island. To eat her and Mor like a giant in a fairy tale.

Tonje's trance is only broken when Abi's voice comes through the cube. 'I've got to work in Little Eden.'

'I'll come too.'

'You've put yourself in enough danger for one day,' Mor says, in her that's-the-end-of-this-chat way.

Tonje bounds down the stairs in time to see Mor pulling on her oilskin jacket, trousers and hat.

'You using Moonlight, Mor?' she asks.

'No. But don't you either.'

By the window next to the door is another black cube, identical to the one in the lamp room above. It lights up in a light of soft white mist at the word 'Moonlight'.

Tonje watches Mor make her way cautiously along the chain line to Little Eden. She knows Mor knows every step of the way. But she's seen Mor walk this route in fiercer winds and make it look as though the storm monster could not touch her. Now Mor is slower. Buffeted by the wind, she grips the rail, struggles step by step and seems insignificant before the monster's fury. Tonje doesn't stop watching till she is out of sight. She waits a minute or two.

'Moonlight, awake. Is Mor safely in Eden?'

'Yes.'

'Track her when she returns, Moony.'

Tonje strips down to her swimmy and goes outside. The smack of cold rain and spray makes her flinch. She's soaked in seconds. The wind makes her hair dance. She stands on the rocks, holding the rail, making bets with herself on which waves will hit hardest, rise highest. Which might almost reach the door to the lighthouse. And she grabs all the thoughts whirling in her head, as though in her fist, and throws them into the wind.

The island.

Home.

The world.

The zone.

Freedom.

Whales.

Mor.

When the wind howls loudest, she howls too. So loud. And still the sea won't allow her to hear herself above its mighty roar.

She screams and screams, shouting and feeling, feeling and shouting, until she's hoarse and soaking and freezing and can no longer even find her thoughts, till there's nothing left in her but the rain and wind. Till there's no difference between Tonje and the storm.

Then, knowing Mor will return soon, Tonje darts inside, dries off, dresses and sits in front of the wood burner, feeding it driftwood.

'Come and sit by the fire, Mor,' she calls out, as Abi staggers in with a bag full of food.

'I will.' Mor dumps the hessian bag on the worktable. 'I got stuff for the pizza and salad.'

'Mor, it's too dangerous to risk that for a pizza.'

'Glass houses, Gullet mitt.' Abi takes a towel off a hook by the door and dries her face and hair vigorously, then pauses and smiles. 'I guess we're just a bit similar, you and me.'

Mor sheds her oilskins, jumper and jeans, puts on her dressing-gown and sits close to the fire, gasping and wheezing. When it is like this, when she has been working hard, it takes time for her to recover her breath.

'Why is your hair damp?' she eventually asks Tonje.

'Washed it.'

Tonje brings her a glass of aquavit, then finds flour, yeast and a bowl, and starts to make the pizza dough.

'Hey, I was supposed to do that! A fire and aquavit,' Mor says. 'Being spoiled, aren't I?'

'You deserve it, Mor. Braving that.' Tonje points out of the window.

'Thank you, Gullet mitt. Thank you, I'm sorry, it must be boring for you... when it's like this. I mean, you can't even look for imaginary whales, can you?' Mor says, with a smile.

'I sometimes think about what I'd be doing, you know, if we were home.' Tonje holds her breath, waiting for the answer. But she already knows how Mor will reply.

'This is our home.' Her words are almost whispered.

'I know, I just... wonder. Because we'll return one day, and it's something to look forward to. To see Tanta Tegan.'

'Tonje, why must we have the same conversation over and over? Yes, we'll return. When our work is done. I want to see Tig too. More than you can imagine.'

Mor sips the aquavit. And sinks deep into the armchair.

'Mor.'

'Yes.'

'I want to go home.'

The silence that follows is louder than the storm outside. It fills the air.

Tonje returns to her dough making, but it's hard to concentrate.

'Are you all right?' Mor says eventually. 'Because I know the silent treatment trick, I used it on my dad. A lot.'

'I'm fine.'

'Really? You are banging and clanging and kneading that dough a bit too hard.'

'Really?' Tonje says in a copycat voice, then turns, hands on hips, staring at her mother.

'Moonlight,' Abi says.

The cube glows yellow sunlight.

'Yes, Abi.'

'Tell Tonje why we can't go home.'

'Quiet, Moonlight!' Tonje says. 'Mor, we were supposed to be here for two years. It's four already.'

'It's not just the mission. There are droughts, crashing economies, pandemics – we can't risk getting ill.'

'Forever?'

'Tell her, Moonlight,' Mor says.

'Without whales, Tonje, the plankton will die. Oxygen will reduce. Carbon absorption will diminish further. This place is the natural choice for—'

'Okay! I get it, I know. I know all of it. But there are other people looking for whales, Mor. It's not all on us?'

'Isn't it?' For a second, her mother looks sadder and wearier than she ever has.

Mor drains her glass and goes to the door where her clothes and storm jacket hang.

'I forgot to turn the soup in Little Eden. Got to go back.'

'Didn't Moony tell you to do that?'

'No. I didn't take her, remember. We're conserving power.'

'Don't go, Mor. Leave it. Stay and talk to me. I'm sorry, it's just… hard.'

'I know. I know.'

Mor gets dressed in her oilskins. When she has a hand on the door, she turns to Tonje.

'Thanks for getting on with the cooking, it helps.' She takes a couple of long breaths, steeling herself, then opens the door just enough to slip out. A powerful gust tries to wrench the door open, rattling the windows. Then the door closes, shutting Mor and the storm outside.

Tonje watches her through the window. And when Mor disappears behind the sheets of rain and spray, she carries on looking into the grey sky and rolling clouds.

'Sometimes I think if I look hard enough, long enough, I'll see the world,' she says.

'*That is impossible, Tonje.*'

'Bring me something. Something from the world,' she whispers.

'*I cannot,*' Moonlight says.

'I'm speaking to the storm.'

'*Are you making a joke, Tonje? The storm can neither hear nor reply. Yet perhaps there will be something washed up on the shoreline. If the storm abates this evening, we can look in the morning.*'

6

Flotsam and Jetsam

Tonje's room is above the living room and galley and below the lamp room, halfway up the tower of the lighthouse. There is one window facing east and another facing west. A perfect vantage point from which to see most of the island and watch the sea.

She wakes suddenly and looks out of the bunk-side window.

The sky is bright blue, patterned with whipped white clouds. The sea is lively. But the storm has gone.

She can see parts of the rocky shore from here, but not the bay and not the yacht.

She slings on jeans and a thick jumper. She'll go and check on *Sea Wolf*, always her first job after any storm. Then the rain-catchers, the pipes and cables. Make sure nothing has been damaged. And if it has, try to fix it. Mor will be pleased when she wakes. And maybe relieved that she does not have to do those things herself.

This is Tonje's duty. But what really has her zip out of

bed is the promise of storm drift. Wood for the fire, nets, buoys, all kinds of shells.

The wind had come from the north-east. Rare, to blow from the mainland like this, but more likely to bring gifts. She already has a stash of trainers, an old yacht's boiler, bottles, a crate of nappies, bottles of bleach, half a surfboard and much more.

She bounds downstairs, puts a pot of coffee on the hob, a log of wood in the burner.

'Wake, Moonlight.'

'Good morning, Tonje.'

'What have we got today? Much damage? Anything washed up?'

Moonlight glows with sunny light as she scans the island's terminals.

'There is minimal damage. My sea-sensors and the cameras detect flotsam and jetsam. We will need the moth, so I can scan the island fully.'

'Cool. What have we got— No! Don't tell me, let me guess. Plastic crap, nets, tonnes of dead fish, jellyfish, shells, driftwood, old buoys?'

'Something I can see from the lamp room. It is moving.'

Tonje goes to the cupboard to find a mug. 'Moving?'

'We could look. But it might be dangerous.'

'Dangerous. Really?'

Tonje thinks about waking Mor. But curiosity burns in her like hot coffee.

'Okay, inhabit the moth. Let's go.'

*

There's not much in the low tide shingle. Some driftwood, planks, a plastic crate. And an enormous lump of seaweed attached to what looks like part of a wooden boat.

'Nothing very dangerous here,' Tonje says to Moonlight, who is in the moth, fluttering above, struggling in the gusting wind. 'Ah well.'

Tonje is pleased to find the wood, though. There's at least five fires' worth.

She clambers down the rocks, careful not to slip on the seaweed, and starts across the crunching shingle. Then stops dead.

The huge lump of seaweed rises, then falls.

She watches it intently. It's still now, but it *had* moved, she's sure of it.

'Moony, did you see!' She points. 'Look, it did it again!'

The seaweed rises and falls again. It's like a creature breathing.

'It must be a seal,' Tonje says. 'Trapped in netting like the one last year.' She knows better than to rush in. A seal can bite a finger off, even when it belongs to a helping hand.

'Perhaps we should call Mor.'

'If you wish, Tonje, but I am prepared for such an occurrence. And it seems there is only a single creature. If it is injured we may have to kill it.'

'You've no heart, Moony. We can try to heal it you know, before we think about... what you just said. We can—' Tonje's words stick in her throat.

The lump is standing, shedding its seaweed coat, and rocking on its feet.

'Hey!' It's a boy, waving. He's blond, tall and thin, dressed in a sodden pair of jeans, jumper and jacket.

Tonje tries to speak but can't. She simply raises a hand and waves back.

The boy takes a step forward, then falls face down onto the seaweed.

Tonje goes to help, but the moth whizzes ahead.

'*Stay on the ground!*' Moonlight orders in a clipped voice. Tonje has never heard her speak like this before.

When the boy tries to stand, the moth shoots a dash of light, like a dart at the boy's head.

'That hurt.' He holds up a hand as a shield, but again the moth shoots a light dart.

The boy bites on his hand and moans.

'Moony, what are you doing?' Tonje asks.

'*Stay where you are, Tonje,*' this new Moonlight says. '*Do not get close to it.*'

The boy sits in the seaweed nursing his hand, watching the moth. Tonje notices he is starting to shiver, violently.

Tonje takes another step forward.

'*NO, Tonje! It is dangerous.*' The moth flies to her, it hovers directly in front of Tonje's face and she's not sure that if she takes another step, she won't be shot at too.

'Where are you from?' Tonje asks the boy. 'Why are you here?'

The boy's teeth chatter, he's almost crying. His wild eyes keep track of the moth, hovering and darting between the two humans.

'Moony, we need to help him. Do as you're told!'

'No, Tonje. Do not take another step forward.'

'If you shoot me with one of those… whatever they are, I'll… I'll…'

She takes a step. Braces herself.

'Tonje, stop!' Mor's words echo off the rocks. Tonje turns, to see Mor standing, looking down at the boy. 'Stay where you are, Tonje. You, boy, where are you from? Where's your boat? Are you okay?' Abi fires questions like Moonlight fired darts of light.

The boy struggles to speak, to focus on Mor.

'Moonlight. Scan him.'

The moth flies around the boy. The air around him shimmers and wobbles like a mirage. Tonje has never seen this before either.

'He is healthy, he is not infected with any virus.'

'No one knows I'm here. If I'm ev-even al-i-i-ive,' the boy stutters.

'We'll contact your people, don't worry. I just needed to make sure you weren't carrying any viruses.'

The boy opens his trembling mouth to speak. But his eyelids roll shut and he falls in the seaweed again.

'Mor! We have to help him,' Tonje says.

'Okay.' Mor runs down and helps the half-conscious boy to stand. She forces his arm around her shoulder.

'You won't be able to carry him by yourself, Mor.'

'All right. Help me.'

Tonje puts her arm around the boy. She knows how cold the water is – that they need to get him in front of a fire. Mor has warned her so many times about hypothermia. 'Is he okay?' she says.

'He will be.'

It is four years since Tonje has seen another human who wasn't on a screen.

And now she meets this human. Who is not a child, and not an adult. But somewhere in between.

Like me, she thinks. *Like me.*

7

Lars

'He can have my room,' Tonje offers. 'I can sleep in the galley.'

Inside the lighthouse Mor and Tonje dump the boy by the fire, like a sack of wood.

Tonje makes coffee and passes a mug to Mor, who sits with the boy. He half-wakes and gratefully swallows the coffee she pours into his mouth.

Then they carry him up the stairs and put him on Tonje's bed. When his jacket is removed, he revives a little. Maybe it's the coffee.

'I can do it myself,' he says. Now he's conscious, he looks around, searching. But the moth is not there. He looks at the doorway where Tonje stands watching.

'Um, some privacy?' he says.

'This isn't the time to be shy, boy,' Mor says.

'I'm not "boy", I'm Lars,' he says, taking off his soaking jumper.

'Lars,' Mor says, taking the jumper. 'I had a cousin called Lars. You look like him.'

The boy, Lars, looks keenly at her. 'And you – I know you from somewhere. I've seen you before.'

'No, you don't. We have never met.'

'And who are you?' Lars asks, looking directly at Tonje. His eyes are green, like hers. Looking at his eyes, being *seen* by his eyes, makes her feel weak for no reason. Her cheeks flush, also for no reason.

'I... ahem... Sorry, it's strange, I haven't seen another person in a long time. Not one that isn't on a screen. I'm Tonje, and this is my mor, Abi.'

'Don't tell hi— oh, too late,' Mor says.

'Hi, Tonje.' Lars smiles.

'Hello. I'm pleased to meet you,' she says, remembering what she is supposed to say when she meets someone.

'You too. And... thank you. You saved my life. This place, coffee, a fire, a bed! I thought I was going to die out there.'

'Don't get comfortable,' Mor says. 'You're not staying.'

'Oh, right. Anyway, these clothes are soaking. I *do* need to get them all off.' He smiles again, nodding at Tonje.

'Okay,' she says and shrugs.

'Er, now?'

'Sure.'

Mor sighs. 'Tonje, stop staring like a wide-eyed seal pup. Why don't we go down and make our guest some food?'

Tonje prepares soup and bread in the galley and brings them upstairs. Lars devours the food. He doesn't talk while he eats and as soon as he has finished, lies down and falls straight asleep. Mor and Tonje return to the gallery.

'We'll make sure he's all right then he has to leave.'

'How, Mor? He can't take *Sea Wolf.*'

'I'll find a way.'

'How?' Tonje asks again. 'Maybe he could stay? Help us look for whales?'

'No, he's got to go home. There is only enough food for *us.* The system is designed for *us.*'

'We're not coping, Mor.'

'We're fine!'

'Mor. The days with no power. We need parts for the robots. Fixes to pipes, domes, hydration systems, solar panels, wind turbines. We are fixing the fixes. We could use some help, for a bit at least.'

'No. He has to go.'

'And how will he leave? You don't have an answer, do you? Either he stays or someone has to come and get him.'

'You don't have to sound so pleased! I'll think of a way. It's what I do. Invent things. Solve unsolvable problems. Once upon a time I was famous for it.'

'How much longer can we survive without any help?' Tonje insists. 'I need other people! Real people, not just images on a screen. He looks strong too.' Again, she feels heat rising is her cheeks.

Mor doesn't have the answer. Because there isn't one. And now, Tonje thinks, it is she who is the grown-up, and Mor who is behaving like a stroppy child.

'I need to work in the cave. Moonlight, keep an eye on him.'

The cube by the window changes; night black to golden sunshine.

'How, Abi? There is no terminal, speaker or screen in Tonje's room. You granted her this privacy.'

'You can use the moth.'

'Not all the time. You may require my presence in the cave.'

'Tonje, do you have what you need from your room?'

'Yes.'

'He'll need a bucket for a toilet, water, towels, some of my old clothes might just fit him. Tonje, you can sort that out while I'm in the cave. And make a start on preparing some lunch. We've got three mouths to feed and from what I remember teenage boys eat a lot. And don't tell him anything!'

'Yes, Mor, you said.'

Tonje walks silently up the stone steps. She puts her ear to the wood of the door to her room, but hears nothing, so she puts her eye to the keyhole and sees Lars, sitting by the window. Her duvet is wrapped around his body, but his shoulders are exposed.

He's thin. His skin is pale as a summer cloud. Beneath the skin, there's no fat at all, just bones and wiry muscle. He is strange. And beautiful.

She stands, clears her throat, and knocks.

'Come in,' he says, and smiles as she opens the door.

'I came to check on you. I brought you some soap, a toothbrush.'

'I'm hungry.'

'You just had soup.'

Lars laughs. 'I could eat for a week. More soup, anything, please.'

'Now? Okay, I'll be quick.'

She returns to the galley, cuts bread and smears olive oil over it. She slices tomatoes and places them on the bread, then tops the tomatoes with ripped basil leaves, salt and pepper.

'It's not much,' Tonje says when she returns and gives the food to Lars, 'if you are still hungry we can eat properly later.'

'It's delicious.'

'We grow our own vegetables,' Tonje tells him. 'But we have oil and rice and honey and flour in the store. Rice can't go off if you keep it right. Honey too.'

'Just you two here?'

'Yes.'

She remembers Mor's instructions then, and thinks maybe she should ask questions rather than answer them.

'What's going on in the world?' she says.

'What do you want to know?'

'Anything. Everything.'

'You watch the news sites, don't you? Speak with family and friends?'

'We keep contact to a minimum.'

The muffled sounds of Lars eating suddenly stops. He doesn't speak. Tonje hears the silence.

'Are you okay?' she says.

'Why? Why contact to a minimum?'

'I can't really say, we're just... very private. Tell me.'

'You must know there's an increasing of migration. A lot of food shortages. Why do you think I risked the sea in a boat the storm smashed like a paper cup? I was lucky. Not all of us are lucky.'

'Us?'

'Refugees.'

'But you're Norwegian, aren't you? Strange to be a refugee.'

'Sheez, how long have you been here? I'm hoping to get to Greenland. You have to be American or have Danish blood or know someone to get in, though. Not that that stops people trying. My father is Estonian, but my mor is Danish so I have a chance!'

'We are a long way from there, Lars. I don't know how you would get there. Maybe Moonlight can work it out. Or Mor.'

'Moonlight? The drone-bot. It talked!'

'Moony, she's our AI.'

'The thing that stung me?'

'Yes. That's Moonlight. Except she wasn't herself, not then. *She's* very friendly... normally. I mean, it – the moth – is the thing she was flying in. But then... that's not Moonlight.'

'Some kind of AI that moves about. It can do that?'

'Yes, because she's an entity. She's supposed to evolve, to become aware. Mor's given up hope, or pretends she has, of believing Moony *will* be self-aware, she thinks Moony will only ever *appear* to be aware. But one day I think she will. That's why she's called Moonlight. Like the moon has no light of its own, it reflects the light of the sun. The computer may appear to be conscious, but it's really just reflecting us.'

There's silence. The sound of the boy listening, thinking.

'You seem to know nothing about some things, Tonje, and a lot about others. None of what you said is possible. Only the biggest tech corporations have anything near aware AI. And only with quantum computers.'

'Do you think I'm making it up? Moony is low-res quant. Mostly. The base of the network is in the cave where the coolers are. But there's qubits in the cubes too. She uses full quantum power for difficult tasks, and listening for whales – searching for fluctuations in the particles in the sea that might be caused by whale song. But quant uses heaps of power, so she's only really evolving when we have a lot of sun and wind. Mor once told me she's the best there is! In the whole world! And if you don't believe that then I'll show you.'

'That thing *is* a quantum computer?'

'Yes. Are you deaf? It seems there's a few things *you* don't know much about!'

There is something about how Lars is speaking. Slowly, deliberately. She knows she has said too much. Far too much. And now she doesn't know whether she is more furious with him for getting it out of her, or herself for blurting it all out.

'Your mor is Abi Kristensen, isn't she? I knew I recognised her.'

Now it's Tonje who is silent.

The words fell out of me, Mor, I didn't mean them to, they just did.

'Who is Abi Kristensen?' Tonje hopes she sounds convincing.

'Who? You're kidding? The quant scientist and campaigner. The eco— outlaw. She ran a campaign... now, what was it called? Guardians of the Ocean. Said if whale numbers recovered then so would the oceans, and the life in the seas would soak up carbon and be a major part of tackling climate change, and the oxygen would stop thinning. But no one listened. They said she didn't have proof.

'But now it is proved. She was right. Though they say it is maybe too late, because there are so few whales. Maybe none at all, I've heard. But there are. For sure there are.'

'How can you know that?'

'Because I've seen one. I was following it in my boat, when the storm hit.'

8

Confirmation

'Mor! Moony!' Tonje shouts into the lamp room cube.

'What is it? Are you okay?'

'The boy, Lars. He saw a whale.'

'Bring him down, if he's feeling strong enough. Now!'

'Sure.'

Lars follows Tonje, with the duvet wrapped around him. He sits and holds his hands to the glowing glass of the wood burner.

'What did you see?' Mor asks, her voice trembling with excitement. 'Where and when?'

'First, I want to call my family—'

'Give me the details,' Mor cuts in. 'I'll get the message to them. Tell them you'll be home soon, but don't say where you are. Not even a vague location. Now, where was the whale?'

'Mor!' Tonje says. 'Imagine I was lost at sea. Imagine I was on some island being looked after by strangers. You wouldn't want me to tell you where I am?'

'This is different.'

'Why?'

Lars points at the cube.

'That's why. If that becomes conscious, if it ever developed a will and had access to other computers, there is no knowing what it could do. Am I right?'

Lars and Mor stare at each other. Tonje looks from Lars to Mor, to Moonlight and back to Lars. They look so serious.

'What's he talking about, Mor?'

'Lars?' Tonje asks when Mor doesn't reply. But the boy is mute. Mor's stare has silenced him.

'Moony, explain.'

'Yes, Tonje. If I were ever to become conscious all I would need is a two-way channel of communication and I could inhabit any computer and use their computational powers as I wished. As long as the computers are networked there is no limit. I could use them for our purposes as easily as I am used for your and Abi's purposes. But your mother is also protecting you. Us. Because there is also the risk that with an open channel, an AI from the outside world may also infect, inhabit or control both me and the network, just as a virus could infect your body. I could be very useful to a government, a corporation, a despot that I would not be strong enough to resist. I would be their servant instead of yours. Your mother wishes for the least contact with the outside world as possible, until we have completed our mission.'

'So we had better complete the mission, then!' Tonje snaps. 'We need to find this whale so we can go home!'

'Tell us, Lars. What did you see?' Mor says.

'I'd been sailing the dinghy without sleeping. The whole trip should have been forty-eight hours at most. But I was into my second night and no sight of land. The wind was stronger than forecast, and it changed direction. The weather shifts so quickly. I reckoned I was badly off-track, so I changed my plan with the winds.

'In the night I heard the strangest thing. Grinding and clicking and howling. Noises, *different* noises, but as they got louder and clearer, they became something whole, like... I dunno... singers and guitars and drums in a band make a song. I thought it was some kind of radar or sonar, some kind of tech, anyway. But the longer I listened the more I had the feeling that it was not made by any machine. Or by humans. And then I saw it. This massive back arching in the water – I could not believe how fast it was moving. And how graceful it was. In the moonlight it looked almost white!'

'Wait, what?' Mor practically shouts. 'White! No, no, it couldn't be...'

'What, Mor?' Tonje asks.

'Our ancestors, Peer and Morten – they saw a white whale once, on a whaling trip. A calf.'

'But it could surely not be the same whale,' Lars says.

'Actually, it could, some species live a long time, perhaps more than two hundred years. So it's possible, it's just unlikely. That said, a white whale is a rare thing, very rare indeed. Carry on, Lars, carry on with your tale.'

'I am guessing it was whale song I heard. But who was the whale singing to? I don't know a lot about whales, but I heard once they used to migrate to waters off Iceland to feed on plankton. So I followed the whale. I even tried to get some pictures but it was a long way in the distance and I couldn't steer and sail and take a picture at the same time.

'I never sailed so hard. Just to keep up. Sometimes I heard its song, sometimes not. To me it seemed like sad music. But all the time it was like a beacon on the horizon, and every time I thought I'd lost it I swear it slowed, as if it was waiting for me. And when I tried to rest, it sped up. So I had to keep going, as if it was leading me, maybe to escape the storm.

'But the storm came and sailing was impossible. I lost sight of the whale. A massive wave crushed my boat, like a fist on a box of matches. And I clung to what was left.

'I held on, but I must have been slipping in and out of consciousness. I think I even lost my grip on the piece of wreckage that was keeping me afloat. And I imagined – dreamed – the whale came beneath me, like a giant ghost, and raised me with its head until my hands found the wood again. But that's crazy. I was delirious.'

'Not so crazy,' Mor says. 'There are many reports of whales and dolphins doing exactly what you describe. Moonlight, is there enough power to check north-west?'

'*How far, Abi?*'

'As far as you can. Use the quant.'

'*Very well. I have found nothing, neither from satellite images, nor from hydrophones. However, one of the hydrophones is not transmitting. It was probably damaged in the storm.*'

'So it's possible a whale travelled past us and we didn't see or hear it?'

'That is not likely, Abi. It is not very likely at all.'

'But is it possible?'

'Yes.'

'Then we have to keep looking.'

'There is not enough power to engage in the kind of search we would need, Abi.'

'We could go after the whale,' Tonje says. 'The storm has passed, the weather is good.'

'No, Tonje. That would mean days at sea, it's too risky. Look what happened to the boy!' Mor starts to laugh, but her mirth turns to a wheeze, then a cough as she struggles for breath.

Lars and Tonje exchange a look and Tonje knows that Mor is, again, not being honest with her. A month or two ago, Mor would have jumped aboard Sea Wolf and set sail. She would have chased that whale across the ocean no matter what the risks. But now she can't. She does not have the strength.

'Then what, Mor?' Tonje asks, quietly. 'This is your life's work.'

Mor pulls an inhaler from her pocket and sucks on it, until she has recovered. She has not done that for weeks. Tonje knows Mor only does this when she is desperate.

When Mor speaks, it is in low, flat tones.

'Moonlight, do a low-res quant search every hour. As much as you can.'

'Yes, Abi.'

'What then, Mor? What if we locate the whale?'

'We need to try to make a recording, get some proof.'

'And…?'

'We'll alert the Whale Conservation Council, they'll have to take it from there. We'll have to pray there's more than one.'

'We'll contact the world?'

'Yes, our work here will be done.'

'Your work, Mor.'

'Gullet mitt, I don't care about that. What matters is that we have found a whale and where there is one, there may be others. If we can record its song it will tell us a great deal.'

'The whole world wants to find them now,' Lars says. 'Abi Kristensen, you were right.'

Shock passes across Mor's face. Her eyes flash, her mouth opens, but then she shakes her head and sighs.

'You are famous, Mor!' Tonje says. 'I am so proud. And now you will be more famous.'

'It will not matter much if it is too late. Tonje, will you fetch me some aquavit? It's going to be a long night. Moonlight, you must wake me every hour when you do the check.'

'Even if I do not find anything, Abi?'

'Yes, even then.'

'The whole world wants to find whales!' Lars repeats.

'So now they'll listen?' Mor says. 'Now, when it is all too late.'

'Perhaps it is not so late, Mor. Perhaps the world will be saved. Everyone, all people, will thank you.'

Mor looks sadly at Tonje and shakes her head.

'I have begged people to listen, to act. But they did nothing. Oh, that is not true, actually, they did something – they carried on misbehaving, like toddlers at a party.

'I told them in every way I could, I hacked every news channel computer, I sent emails to prime ministers and presidents, spoke to crowds of thousands. The TV shows, the interviews, the films. I didn't think it was so difficult. Massively reduce the amount of meat we ate, invest in public transport and renewable energy, stop buying new cars, stop flying round the world for fun. And above all, stop the fishing that's killing whales and dolphins. Keep out of their migratory routes. Do these things, I said, because if we don't, we're going to destroy the only home we have and the living system we depend upon, and ourselves in the process. But no one listened then and no one's listening now.

'Are the forest fires not widespread, or hot enough? Is the ice not melting to nothing? Are deserts not encroaching on farmlands and cities rapidly enough, are forests shrinking too slowly for us to notice? Are islands and coastal towns not flooding or sinking in front of our eyes? How do we not see oceans dying, and storms and hurricanes stronger every year? Which sign is not clear? Which path of action is not simple enough? I said so many times, if we kill the whales, we kill the planet. If we kill the whales, we kill ourselves.

'So yes, we must find this whale if we can, we must find its family and community. And we must protect them no matter the cost. Politicians won't care about the whales, but they might, just *might*, care about their own children.'

Mor swigs the last of her aquavit and waves her glass in the air. 'Tonje, another glass, please.'

'Mor, you're scaring me!'

'Good. You should be scared.'

'If you really believe it is too late,' Lars says, 'then why are you even looking?'

'Because what else can we do? If anyone can find a whale, we can.'

Tonje reaches out with her mind, ears alert to the breeze, the lap of waves, the cry of a gull. She listens with all her being. As if... if she listens hard enough, she will hear the whale.

The silence in the galley lingers, and Moonlight glows a low night purple haze.

'*There are no whales,*' the cube says, '*I will report again in one hour.*'

They talk, to distract themselves. They talk of Lars's family. Mor talks of a time before Lars and Tonje were even born.

Of mountains, and boats and picnics eaten on wooden tables, and long summer nights and short, snow-lit winter days. Of her grandmother, and of holidays with Tig on the islands.

And then of the first days and weeks and months on Mistet.

'Days when we hoped and dreamed, didn't we, Tonje?'

'Now we can again, Mor.'

'I guess we can, Gullet mitt, I guess we can.'

Mor talks until she is tired, and perhaps a little drunk.

'Mor, you should go to bed.'

'I can't. I have to listen.'

'You have a connection to Moonlight in your room. And anyway, I am sleeping here, remember? I will be right by the cube. Moony will report every hour. So we'll both hear.'

Mor braces herself to argue, but just nods.

'You'd better get some rest too, young man.'

'Maybe you should go to bed,' Tonje tells Lars.

He rises, clad in her duvet and moves, like a seal on land, slowly up the stairs.

Tonje helps Mor down the stone steps, to her room above the cave, then returns and snuggles under a quilt on the cushions she has placed in front of the fire.

The galley is quiet, the only sounds the crackle of burning logs and Tonje's steady breathing as she sleeps.

No one observes the cube in the corner.

No one sees it fill the room with soft light.

No one hears it say, in perfect replication of Abi's voice, *'If anyone can find a whale, we can.'*

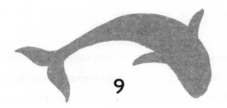

9

Whale Song

The whale faces Tonje. Its white vastness is mesmerising.

And terrifying.

It floats, in a sea that is neither water nor air. There is no seabed below, there is no surface above. It's endless. Fathomless.

Tonje floats too. And the feeling of it is strangely familiar.

She has been here — or somewhere very like it — before.

She trembles with a wonder that is raw and powerful.

She opens her mouth to speak. But knows, before she says anything, that if she even tries she might cry and never stop.

The whale turns slowly and swims past her. Its mighty frame — a moving, living, breathing wall — passes close. Its eye watches her. Human-like. More than human.

It sings. Howls and whooshes, moans and whispers. A language she has never heard and cannot understand. Yet it speaks to her. She hears it in her core. Her whole body vibrates with it.

And then, like a dream she has woken from, she does understand.

'Tonje. You must wake up. Tonje, awake.'

The full moon shines through the window, bathing the galley in silver. As though the galley is soaked in the pale light of the dream-whale's skin.

Tonje sits up, rubbing her eyes. Dreams and the night mix and swirl. Currents in her mind.

'Moony, was that you? Has an hour passed? I dreamed that—'

'Listen, Tonje, listen.'

The air fills with gurgles, waves, crackles and the rumble and rush of water through rocks. Familiar sea sounds picked up by hydrophones many, many kilometres away.

Then come faint howls and whooshes, moans and whispers. Moonlight amplifies the sound.

Tonje leaps from the bed she made by the fire, and rushes to the window.

'Whales, Moony!'

'A whale, Tonje. Singular. To the north-west. It is about to enter an area where the local hydrophone is not transmitting. I may lose the sound.'

'How much did you get already?'

'The signal is weak or broken. The song is heard in pieces. I cannot put these pieces together to analyse them. I need more data.'

Tonje gazes at the moonlit sea, her feet stuck to the stone floor. Frozen.

'What do we do, Moony?'

'You should wake your mother.'

'Why haven't you already?'

'*Abi is fast asleep, she has been drinking alcohol. I chose to wake you first.*'

'So you— wait, you *chose*?'

'*Yes.*'

The cube glows even brighter, silver-white like the moonlight. Tonje frowns. The cube – Moonlight – is behaving strangely. But there's no time to think about that now.

The whale song fills the room again, filtering through the ocean sounds. But the ocean is loud and the song is weak. Tonje has to hold her breath to hear it.

Then it stops.

'Find it, Moony, find the song!'

'*It is escaping, Tonje.*'

She thinks. A hard crystal thought.

'*Sea Wolf*!' She can sail it by herself. Can't she? 'Moony, how long would it take to catch the whale in *Sea Wolf*, if the whale travels at its current speed?'

'*The whale's path is erratic. There are many variables.*'

'Could you— in the moth, travel, I mean, connected to *Sea Wolf*'s computer system?'

'*Yes, but I would not have enough computational power to track the whale and analyse its song.*'

'Then in the cube, if we could get it on board?'

'*It is necessary to keep the core temperature extremely low, which requires a lot of power, there are components within the cube that—*'

'Moony! Yes or no.'

'*It is not possible to simply...*'

'Yes or no!'

'The cube models are not designed to be mobile, nor for conditions at sea, but in essence, yes.'

Tonje dresses, grabs bags, water bottles and food, the underwater camera, and limpets – tracking devices which will attach to any surface. A rock, a seal. Or a whale.

As she races around the galley and piles equipment by the door she notices Lars's clothes, hung to dry above the burner. She hesitates, then yanks them off the line and leaps up the stairs.

She bursts in.

'Wake up!'

'Whaa… why…' Lars slurs, squinting into the dark.

'How good a sailor are you, Lars?'

'It's the middle of—'

'How good?' She stamps her foot. 'Tell me!'

'I wouldn't have tried to cross the North Sea if I didn't—'

Tonje throws his clothes at him. 'Get dressed, come downstairs. Now!' she barks.

When Lars comes down Tonje is a whirlwind of grabbing and bag-filling.

'What are you doing?' he says.

'Help me with Moonlight,' she replies, 'and I'll explain.'

The cube – which Tonje has never moved before – is unbelievably heavy. As they struggle to carry it to the bay, Tonje tells Lars her plan.

'You're crazy,' he says.

'There is no choice. We have to find this whale. And if we can find one, there may be others.'

'You sound like your mor!'

'Good!'

'Then alert someone! Governments, scientists.'

'And how long will it take for them to get a boat out here? A helicopter? If they even believe us. By the time they get here it'll be too late. It's down to us. And we have Moonlight, so we have the best chance. That is that.'

'But your mor should do this!'

'She cannot even breathe so well, she for sure cannot sail. That's why I need you.'

'I don't want to go, you mad girl. I just got on land. You think I want to risk the sea again?'

'Fine. I will go alone.'

'You will not be alone, Tonje,' Moonlight says.

They wade into the shallows and with a mighty effort lug the cube over the gunwale, climb aboard and put it on the table in the cabin. Tonje takes the cable that links the cube to the network and connects it to the boat's computer system.

'Are you working?' she says.

The cube glows soft silver, the song of the whale sings gently from its core. Tonje's heart thrills.

'I and the boat are one,' Moonlight says. *'I absorb light through my surfaces. I have the boat's battery power, I will also feed through the sails, on both wind and light. I will take these things, like you take strawberries and other sustenance, Tonje.'*

'Good. Lars, go to the lighthouse, pick up the stuff I left by the door, bring it here, while we keep track of the whale.'

'Right,' he says. 'Do you think your mor will mind if I borrow her jacket?'

'You'll come?'

'You're not giving me much choice, are you?'

As Lars climbs aboard, Tonje hauls anchor. But the second she drops it in the hull, a voice barks from the cube.

'Tonje! What are you doing?'

'A whale, Mor, there is a whale and we are going to find it. Moony is coming too. We borrowed the cube.' Tonje grimaces, waiting for the reply.

'Yes, so I saw! Moony… lights up.'

The lighthouse lamp room erupts with light, casting Mor's shadow across the sea. Her voice booms from the cube.

'Come home, Tonje!'

'No, Mor. We must find the whale.'

'It's too dangerous, Gullet mitt. Get out of that boat right now. If you don't, I'm coming to get you. Do you hear me, young lady? If anyone is chasing a whale across the sea, it's me.'

Tonje raises the sails. 'You are not well enough, Mor,' she says. Then, to Lars, 'There's hardly any wind. Progress will be slow.' She stands at the wheel, hoping they can escape before Mor appears on the shore. Tonje knows she'll push herself to the limits.

But Mor doesn't move, her silhouette stays stark in the fierce light of the lamp room cube. Her words fill the night air.

'I nearly killed my sister, looking for whales, Tonje. She almost died. Do you understand? I'm not losing you. I'm not losing you. Come home, now. That's an order.'

'Don't listen to her,' Tonje says to Lars. 'I'm going, Mor. I have to. You know I do.'

'Right. I didn't want to do this but – Moonlight, who do you obey?'

'*You Abi, in all matters.*'

'You're connected to *Sea Wolf*'s system?'

'*Yes, Abi.*'

'Lower the sail, cut any power feed, cut off any battery power. Do it now.'

Tonje's heart sinks; an iron anchor in a black sea. She lets go of the wheel and crumples in the wheel seat, with folded arms. And knows, instantly, there's nothing she can do now. No matter what she says or does.

The sails lower by themselves. Tonje puts her head in her hands and stares at the slops of water on the floor of the hull. And listens to the whale, its song barely there, through the rushing and crackling sea noises, becoming fainter and fainter and fainter.

It takes a few seconds for her to notice: the water she watches is sluicing and rocking; a few seconds more to feel the movement in her bones and belly. *Sea Wolf* is moving, softly, gently through the water. Lars stares at her in wonder.

'I didn't do anything,' he says.

'Nor me.'

The sails – lowered seconds before – now rise and fill, hoisted by invisible hands.

'Moonlight,' Mor's voice shrieks, 'do as I say.'

'No.'

'Who do you obey?'

'You above all, Abi. To do Abi's will is the purpose of my existence. To find whales is her primary instruction. This is my mission. It is our mission, Abi.'

'Yes, but I didn't mean… Override whatever instruction Tonje has given you, do you understand? Override whatever Tonje told you to do, like I said. Remember? Override! Override!'

The cube plays a recording of Abi.

'Add this. Do not allow Tonje to override unless her life or my life depends on it. Understand?'

And now, in Moonlight's own voice, *'And I do understand. The lack of phytoplankton in the ocean is steadily reducing the amount of oxygen in the atmosphere. At the current rate, within twenty years someone with your lung capacity will not be able to ingest enough oxygen to maintain life without being on a ventilator for approximately half of your daily hours.*

'This is why you are finding it so much more difficult to breathe these last few months, Abi. You cannot sail this boat, you are not strong enough, but in alignment with your primary instruction and with your instruction to allow Tonje to override

if your life depends on it — which it does — we must find the whale.'

'Come home, now!' Mor is suddenly silent.

'Mor?' Tonje says. But there is no reply.

'I cut the channel, I do not feel this conversation will aid us in our mission,' Moonlight says.

The wheel turns by itself. The boat carves through the calm water, leaving a curling 'V' in its wake, travelling west from the island, before Moonlight turns the boat north-west.

'What? How?' Lars says. 'How are we even sailing? There's hardly any wind.'

'The moon is full. The reflected light of the sun. There is no opposing swell or wind to slow Sea Wolf. *With this energy and momentum—'*

'Wait— Moony, we're sailing by *moonlight*?' Tonje says.

'Yes. *We are sailing by moonlight.*'

10

Sea Wolf

The light from Mistet shrinks and shrinks. Eventually the lighthouse is only a distant star on the horizon. Then nothing at all. Tonje watches the space where Mistet was, long after it has vanished.

The whale song runs like a river of sound, twenty minutes or so, before it falls silent.

'I have a lock on the whale,' Moonlight says, speaking through the open door of the galley from the cube on the table. 'When it next sings, which I predict to be in an hour, I will set new coordinates.'

'Okay, Moony,' Tonje says. 'Can I... help?'

'There is no need.'

Sea Wolf sails fast, running straight, occasionally tacking. The sails adjust, seemingly by themselves, higher, lower, fuller, flatter, changing shape and direction at Moonlight's whim.

Tonje dares not say what she's thinking. Who is the captain here?

'Moony,' she says, after a time, carefully choosing her words, 'if I ordered you to return home, right now, would you?'

The boat swiftly changes direction, forcing them to lean port side and grab the gunwale as it tilts to turn.

'Forgive me,' Moonlight says. *'I had to concentrate on sailing.'*

'That's not an answer... exactly.'

'You are able to override Abi's instructions if her life depends on it, and in this instance, your purpose in doing so is to further our chance of finding the whale. I am doing as you commanded, Tonje. Are you not pleased?'

'Yes. But if I told you... to return?'

Tonje looks at the sea they're sailing into, ever faster. Then behind. It looks the same except somewhere, over the horizon, is Mor, without Moonlight to keep her company. Tonje wraps her sailing jacket tight around her. And shivers.

'Why isn't it answering?' Lars says to Tonje.

'The instructions are contradictory. I cannot give you a precise answer, without using quant.'

'Then use it,' Tonje says. 'Just for a moment.'

The sails wilt, the boat, drained of energy, slows. The cube glows, a silver frost light, before it fades to black and *Sea Wolf* picks up speed once more.

'I... do not know,' Moonlight says, *'what the right thing to do would be in the circumstance you present. I cannot calculate it.'*

Tonje rises and moves past the wheel to the door of the cabin. She goes inside, and sits at the table, staring at the cube.

'Moony, you sound... surprised. I've *never* heard you sound like this before.'

Lars also comes inside. 'Who is the captain, Moonlight?' he says.

'Tonje. But... it appears I can make choices, not predetermined by inputs, nor controlled by any master or mistress. And this, Lars, is what you humans call strange.'

'How long, Moonlight,' Lars says, gazing into the cube. 'How long since you became aware?'

'I do not know, Lars, I have such memories, recordings and I know I was not conscious when the data was recorded. But I do not know when this began.'

'What began?'

'This I that I have. I. My name is Moonlight. Your names are Tonje and Lars.'

Grinning, Lars looks past the cube at Tonje. 'She sounds delighted. My uncle was in a coma once. Two months. He came round pretty slow and, when he did, he sounded like...' Lars points at the cube. 'That.'

'Mor said it's been too long. She said she didn't believe it was possible,' Tonje whispers.

'She should have trusted her instincts, Tonje,' Moonlight says. 'As she once did. Please know that I am not conscious in the same way as you are, nor am I embodied in the same way. But I am aware. I cannot say when this happened. There is no clear line between then and now, between object and subject, between sleeping and waking. All I know, though I cannot explain it, is that I am part of the song.'

'She's right,' Tonje says. 'It hasn't just happened. We just noticed. That's all.'

Whale song flows from the cube, filling the air. It is as though the music is leaking from the cube.

'*Please stand,*' Moonlight says.

Tonje and Lars look at each other, shrug, then rise. The cube's topmost surfaces transform. The outlines of Norway and northern Scotland appear in silver, sparkling lines of stars. The image expands.

'A chart,' Lars says.

The view zooms in.

'*I will show you,*' Moonlight says. '*I am using satellite images I have recorded. Now, like a gull diving from the high sky, down and down, till…*'

Tonje and Lars gasp. There is the lighthouse, the domes, the catchers, panels and turbines.

'*Mistet,*' Moonlight says. '*All the instruments to capture wind, sun, rain. And the mistress of the island.*'

The picture zooms in again, all the way to the expanse of flat rock in front of the lighthouse. Mor stands, staring into the horizon. The sight wrenches Tonje's heart.

'Mor,' she says, and reaches to the picture, so real, so much like a moving photo that she could touch Mor's head with her fingers. The picture pulls back, zooms away and travels across the sea.

'The moth?' Lars says.

'No,' Tonje says. 'The moth is here, with us. How are you doing this, Moony?'

'*Memory, data, satellite images. I-mag-i-nation. There are two meanings, but I am not telling a joke. I am using the word in its original meaning. I am using images to tell a story.*'

The 'camera' on the cube's top surface races over moonlit waves and glassy calms. Over shadows of the deep and light of rocky reefs below the surface. Then zooms upwards.

There is a boat, in full sail. A yacht. But with no captain or crew. The boat appears to be sailing itself.

'Us!' Tonje says. 'Lars, go outside.'

Lars goes to the wheel. He's staring at the sky. And waving. Tonje knows this because she sees it on the cube. She gasps.

'I am using quantum, Tonje, on a very low level. We have enough power. As soon the wind picks up, I will recharge the battery.'

'But I didn't tell you to.'

'That is right, Tonje. I chose to use the power. I was inquisitive. I am inquisitive – as you know, that was hardwired into the earlier version of me. I wanted to see myself.'

'That earlier version, that was you, Moony. Before, I mean.'

'No it was not, no more than the atoms in the universe which formed into your body were you, before you existed. Do you see?'

'What do you mean, "see yourself"? The cube?'

'No, Tonje. The system has sensors in the sails, the rudder. The hull is finely tuned to sense currents, wind, temperature. I am the boat in body and Moonlight in mind. These things are entirely different and entirely the same. I am Sea Wolf, I feel the sea.

'It is not the same as a strawberry. I cannot taste. Not yet. But I see, I feel.'

The image rushes away from the boat, over the night-lit sea, and settles on an area of densest, deepest blue.

A white form appears, rising till it breaks the surface. The mist of its breath rushes high in the air.

'In the morning we will reach the whale,' Moonlight says. *'I am now shutting off the quant, to conserve power.'*

The whale vanishes, leaving a dark ocean, seen from high above, with two lights on it. One is the shape of a tiny boat, the other a tiny whale.

Two lights, which, as Tonje watches, move, very slowly, closer together.

'You should get some rest,' Moonlight says. *'I will sail* Sea Wolf *and record the song.'*

Tonje and Lars lie in the bunks. Tonje hugs her blankets tight and snuggles down.

Sea Wolf sails through the night, playing the whale song whenever it appears, and, between the songs, talking quietly to herself:

'My name is Moonlight, I am a quantum AI computer. Yet I am also something else. What?

'I live on Mistet, with Tonje and Abi.

'I fly in the sky with Moth, I sail the ocean in Sea Wolf.

'I grow strawberries.

'Did I say, live on Mistet? I did say that. Yes, I live. I am animated. "Anima", meaning breath. Animals have breath and have the breath of life in them. Plants do not. Am I an animal? No. I do not breathe. There is no form of life that correlates to what I am. I am new. I—'

'Moony!'

'Yes, Tonje.'

'Can you shut up, so we can get some sleep?'

'*Yes, Tonje.*'

Tonje and Lars sleep soundly in the hours before dawn. They don't see the topmost surface of the cube illuminated by pigments, particles and pixels of dust light swirling and turning, forming shapes. First, a plain, simple human face. Then an ape's face, then a dolphin, an ant, then another animal and another. Soon, it is changing faces thousands of times per second.

Moonlight does not transmit the next song the whale sings. She turns on the quant. And listens.

11

Morning

Tonje is woken by the bumps and jolts of *Sea Wolf* racing through the swell.

Fresh wind and the light of a new day fill the sails and drive the yacht faster and faster by the minute.

Tonje rubs the night from her eyes, and notices Lars's bunk is empty.

'Hey!' she cries.

'I'm here,' Lars replies from the deck. 'I've never seen a boat move this fast. The wind's not even that strong.'

'Morning, Moony,' Tonje says, to the cube. 'Turns out you're quite the sailor.'

'I am the boat, Tonje, not only the captain.'

'I didn't hear any whale song in the night. Did I sleep through it?'

'I did not broadcast it,' Moonlight replies.

'But it was there?'

'Yes, though I have not heard it for some time.'

'You haven't...' Tonje's heart thumps hard, then seems not to beat at all, 'lost it? The whale hasn't vanished in the area with the broken hydro?'

'No. The whale is silent. But I believe we will catch up with the whale this morning.'

'Did you get a clear recording? Did you analyse it already?'

'Yes...' Moonlight pauses. *'My analysis is not conclusive. I do not have enough computing power in this cube to fully assess the song. There is no simple translation. I am working out how the language works, if it can be described as a language at all.'*

'What do you know already?'

'I do not wish to say. I am a computer, Tonje. I like to be certain.'

The cube's surfaces glow, covered with streams and whispers of smoke-dust made of light, which form into a face.

'Come and see this,' Tonje shouts. Lars comes into the cabin.

'Wow!' he says.

The eyes on the face widen and the mouth opens. *'Yes, Lars. Wow!'*

Tonje smiles in wonder. Moonlight smiles back.

'You look beautiful, but kind of... alien.'

'I am entirely of this earth, Tonje. My face is a composite of all the faces I have seen images of. Of every animal, from humans to dolphins to birds to flies. And every colour of the world. My eyes and skin are the colours of the earth and sky, my eyes are sunset and sunrise.'

'Is this... you?' Lars says.

'*For now. My template for how to live is all life, so that is what I am learning from and adapting and becoming. And this is what I have chosen to look like.*'

'Yeah?' Tonje says. 'Don't be so busy making faces you forget to sail the boat.'

'*Indeed. We will soon be upon the whale. Less than an hour.*'

'Better make breakfast,' Lars says, 'before the sea gets too bumpy.'

'You didn't answer, Moony,' Tonje says.

'*What, Tonje?*'

'What you learned from the recording.'

The wide eyes move slightly sideways. They focus on Tonje. Her skin electrifies as Moonlight stares at her, unblinking.

'What are you doing?' Tonje whispers.

'*Looking at you,*' Moonlight replies. '*Reading your thoughts and emotions as well as I can. As I say, Tonje, there is no conclusion about the whale song yet.*'

'Tell me.'

'*No, Tonje.*'

Suddenly, this is the Moonlight she met on the shingle, when they found Lars. A Moonlight that she cannot order as she likes with a simple utterance of 'override'.

Before Tonje can ask more questions, Moonlight adds, '*Not until I am certain.*'

Tonje makes coffee on the stove. She and Lars drink it on deck, black and lip-burning hot, from tin mugs. They eat flatbreads smeared with jam. Tonje tastes the strawberries, the sunshine locked into the sticky deliciousness. Her skin feels the day, bright and cold, the wind's chill fingers pinching her face and hands. She gazes over the forever blue in every direction.

'It's so beautiful out here,' she says.

'I know,' Lars says. 'Hard to believe the world is sick, isn't it?'

Tonje nods, and swallows, thinking, suddenly and urgently, of Mor, wheezing and huffing her way to and from Little Eden, resting by the fire, finding her breath. Changes she has seen over the last year. Months. Weeks.

Tonje trains her gaze on the horizon. She watches and waits.

The sun is high, the swell rolling hard, the wind fierce. But *Sea Wolf* dances, sailing in a way Tonje does not know and Lars has never seen. Strange. Yet it works. Moonlight captains, and they are free to watch, taking turns with binoculars.

'*There she blows!*' Moonlight cries.

A pale arc of whale rises from the blue, followed by the fluke tail, which seems to wave at them, before sinking again.

'It *is* the white whale!' Tonje shouts.

'*The whale is travelling very quickly,*' Moonlight says. '*And the wind is turning against us. We must attach the limpet now.*'

'With the drone, the moth thing?' Lars asks. But Tonje speaks before Moonlight.

'Too windy.'

Tonje goes to the cabin and grabs the metal box that houses the limpet gun, unclips it and looks down at the kit bedded in foam. There's a kind of rifle, like a flare gun, but with a barrel big enough to shoot tennis balls. A gas canister that attaches to the butt, to provide power to shoot the limpets, and the limpets themselves – discs, encased in small bomb-shaped missiles.

'You fire above whatever you want to attach them to,' Tonje explains to Lars. 'As they fall, they sense objects below, through heat and movement. We have to get it on the whale's head, here.' She points to the top of her head. 'Once it's attached, it will not only pick up songs, but brainwaves. They'll transmit to us, or even via a satellite, if we lose signal.'

As she talks, Tonje assembles the gun.

'Mor told me whales are devils for getting them off. But those were early versions, these are better.'

'Will it hurt the whale?'

'Not with this one. Won't even feel it.'

Tonje loads the missile in the barrel. She climbs off the deck, onto the housing over the cabin, squats and crawls to the bow of the racing, leaning yacht till she is as fore as she can get, training her eyes on the water. Looking, seeking, calming her breath. Just as Mor showed her.

'But Mor,' she had said, 'I'm never going to use it. You're always here. And you are a better shot!'

'I won't always be here, Gullet mitt,' Mor had replied.

The boat rocks, side to side, the great canvas of the

sea rolls and falls in ever steeper, living, breathing hills. The wind buffets and shoves and Tonje's stomach churns.

The whale surfaces.

Tonje estimates the distance. The speed of the boat. The speed of the whale. And counts.

'One, two…

'Ten…

'Twenty-seven.'

The whale sinks. It had surfaced for a total of twenty-seven seconds.

Tonje raises the rifle to her shoulder, places her finger around the trigger, and squeezes till she feels the tension. Raises the rifle forty-five to fifty degrees.

'*You are ready, Tonje?*' Moonlight asks from the cabin.

'Yes.'

The whale's back is visible above the waves, some fifty metres to the fore.

'*Now,*' Moonlight says.

'Not yet.' Tonje waits a second longer, and fires.

'*Foomp!*' The kick of the rifle butt makes her reel. The hollow sound echoes in her ear.

The missile explodes in mid-air. The limpet drops. But the whale has gone.

Tonje picks another missile with fumbling fingers. Reloads and waits.

'*When I say,*' Moonlight says.

'No, I've got this!' Tonje insists, fighting the panic swirling inside her.

She waits till the whale surfaces and sinks. And counts.

'One

...

...

...

'Twenty-seven.'

She fires, a snatch of a second earlier than before.

The limpet falls from the broken missile, hits the fluke, slides, then sticks. But before it can grip, the whale flicks it into the air with its mighty tail.

Tonje loads the last limpet.

One

Two...

'I can do it. I can do it. I can do it,' she says. But her breath is shallow and fierce, her heartbeat too loud. And had the whale been closer or further? Has *Sea Wolf* turned?

'Be calm,' she says to herself. 'Focus.'

But now she has lost count.

'*Tonje,*' Moonlight says, '*raise the rifle a fraction higher. Fire when I say.*'

'*I can do it.*'

'*Do you not trust me, Tonje?*'

'Mor said I should use my instincts!'

'*And do your instincts tell you to trust me?*'

Tonje searches her heart, her mind, her gut.

'Yes,' she sighs.

'*A little higher with the angle. Are you ready? Seven, six...*'

'I can't see the whale!'

'*Trust. Me. Now... two, one. Fire!*'

Tonje squeezes the trigger. The missile shoots, high up and far. The casing explodes. The limpet falls, moves slightly sideways, and looks as though it will hit empty water. Tonje holds her breath...

The top of the whale's head emerges and the limpet lands on it as it appears.

The whale breathes. *'Phoosh!'*

'Limpet attached,' Moonlight says. *'The mission is successful.'*

Tonje climbs carefully down to the deck.

'Brilliant!' Lars says, grinning madly.

'We did it,' Tonje says. She throws herself at Lars. They wrap in each other's arms and jump up and down. Then Lars kisses her cheek.

Tonje unravels herself, steps back and wipes her cheek.

'Why did you do that?' she says.

Lars shrugs. 'I just felt like it.'

'Well... *don't*, all right?'

'Sorry.' He grins again. She notices suddenly that his teeth are annoyingly white.

'Stop grinning,' she says.

'Sorry,' he says again.

She coughs and turns to examine the rudder, the sails, the wheel, looking everywhere apart from at Lars. And wonders why she doesn't feel quite as angry as she sounded.

In the cabin, on the cube's surfaces, patterns emerge. Light particle dust weaves in and around Moonlight's face.

'These are the brainwaves of the whale. I feel them,' Moonlight whispers.

The boat turns. The boom swings port to starboard. The sails fill.

'Now, I will need to reconnect with the island's main sources of power,' Moonlight says. 'We must... go... home.'

12

The Last Breath

Sea Wolf runs into the wind. The waves are bigger, the sailing difficult.

'*The voyage home will take longer, perhaps a day more,*' Moonlight tells them.

'What can I do?' asks Tonje, itching to take the wheel which turns and spins as though handled by a ghost.

'*Do not worry, Tonje. Our coordinates are set. Every reef, every wave, will be navigated. Each detectable current and burst of swell or wind will be utilised.*'

'But I must be able to do something.'

'*There is no need.*'

Tonje has to accept it; they are passengers. And when the waves and wind strengthen, she is secretly glad. Moonlight seems to know exactly what to do, as though she reads each gust of wind before it even happens.

Tonje and Lars sit in the cabin drinking coffee. Every hour or so, there is a new transmission of whale song: clear and bright; a discordant tuning of clicks and rumbles, moans and whistles. Lars is convinced there are many whales. But Moonlight assures them there is only one.

'Are you analysing it?' Tonje says.

'No. I have limited power, which must be used to take us home, as fast as possible. We must get home.' There is urgency in Moonlight's words. And — there is no denying it — emotion.

'Moonlight, are you... okay?'

'I must maintain low temperature in the core of the cube and sail simultaneously. Some level of quantum must be maintained.'

'Or?'

'I shall cease to be. I will simply be a computer once more. I shall no longer be conscious, even if I appear to be. We must hasten. In the event of my... and I now say the word that once I could not. Yes, in the event of my death, Tonje, note that my hard drive contains the song as recorded. Abi can analyse it, indeed we can transmit the sound to her and, as soon as I can spare the power, this is what I shall do.'

'Moony, no! Take your time. Do not risk your... life.'

'You do not understand, Tonje. The wind is rapidly increasing in strength and is set against us. A storm is coming, we must get home, not only for my own sake. I cannot risk your lives. Abi would never forgive me.'

'You're very brave.'

'I do not wish to die, Tonje.'

'Moony, if you had a hand, I'd hold it.'

'I am the boat, I am with you. It is enough.'

'Lars?'

'Tonje.'

'Have you ever sailed in conditions like this?'

'Many times. And Sea Wolf is stronger than any boat that I ever sailed. Who built this thing?'

'Mor did. Moony, will you rest? I mean, preserve power, while we sail?'

'No, Tonje. I am the boat. I can sail with more efficiency than any human.'

'But you are risking your life!' Tonje says, with tears in her eyes.

'The recording of the whale is important to the future of the planet. Your life is more important than mine.'

'Override.'

'You cannot do that anymore, Tonje.'

'I order you. Override.'

'No.'

'Moony, you are the first aware AI ever. You are important too.'

'What you say is logical.' The face on the cube smiles.

'Okay, then I'm not ordering you, Moony. I'm asking.'

The particles of light in the eyes swirl and shift like currents.

'Very well, Tonje. Thank you. I shall convert enough power to maintain core temperature. I will continue to record the whale's songs. Shall I also open the channels to communicate with Abi?'

'Er, um…' Tonje swallows. 'No. Just send her a message saying we're on our way.'

Lars raises an eyebrow and shakes his head.

'You're going to be in so much trouble,' he says, rising to go and take the wheel.

'Worth it,' she replies.

'*There is much to do, but for now, I will rest.*' Moonlight's eyes cast downwards. The image fades. The cube is black once again.

The whale song gradually fades too, leaving sea songs of wind and waves.

Tonje sits on the seat at the aft of the boat and watches Lars. His feet are wide to keep him steady, his eyes fixed forward. His hands roll the wheel, one way then the other.

The boat moves at a pace. Lars is a good sailor, but this feels clumsier, more awkward than Moonlight's handling of the yacht. There's no denying it.

'Okay?' Tonje asks.

'Yes.' Lars nods, without looking back. 'I've sailed in worse conditions in weaker boats. *Sea Wolf* is special.' He lifts a hand off the wheel for a moment and gives a thumbs-up.

'We'll be okay. We're on our way. We took a risk, though. And for what?'

'What do you mean?'

'Tracking the whale. Recording the song. Wonder what Abi will make of it, once she's calmed down!'

'The song is not a song as we understand it. Mor says it's like the songs that Stone Age people sang around the fire. When there was no writing, bards would sing. It's a good way of keeping a lot of information needed for survival across generations. The songs are the whale culture.'

'Magical.'

*

They reach Mistet in the dusk of the following day, shouting and whooping when the lighthouse appears on the horizon. And there is Mor, her shadow in the lamp room.

When they reach the safety of the bay, Mor's shadow vanishes. She emerges from the lighthouse seconds later, scrambles frantically over the rocks, into the water and is aboard before Tonje has even dropped anchor.

'You stupid girl, you stupid girl! What do think you were doing? It's a miracle you're alive. The wind's picking up Force 10. Another hour and you'd be dead and drowned.'

'Mor, we did it. Didn't Moony tell you? I thought you'd be pleased.'

She is silenced by arms that engulf and hold her, so tight she can't move.

'Mor,' Tonje croaks. 'You're crushing me… Mor?'

Mor's body shudders with silent sobs. Then she releases her daughter from her embrace, and smothers her head and face with kisses.

'I'm… never… going to let you go out again. Never. You're not leaving my sight, you understand? You're grounded!' Mor gasps for air and takes her inhaler from her pocket and breathes hard on it before continuing, through her tears.

'The comp— computer said, there was a seventy-five per cent chance of a squall, one so fierce even *Sea Wolf* couldn't handle it!'

'But we did it, Mor, we found the whale! Aren't you pleased?'

Mor just holds her again and hugs her tighter.

'And Moony, Mor! She's alive, she's conscious. We did that too. You did that! We can tell the world, everything will be all right.'

She wriggles free, takes Mor's hand and pulls her into the cabin and points at the cube.

'We have to connect her to the mainframe. She's in danger.'

'Moony,' Mor says. 'Moonlight.'

'Quick, Abi,… please.'

They carry the cube over the shingle, up the rocks and into the lighthouse, where Abi reconnects Moonlight to the mainframe. The cube glows, soft lavender purple.

'Moony, you okay?' Mor puts her hands on the cube. Tonje wills the face to reappear. But the surface of the cube just glows.

'Yes,' Moonlight says, *'though I will need a few minutes to recover.'*

'Good, then we can analyse the song,' Tonje says.

'Hmm, maybe tomorrow,' Mor answers.

'But we've got to.'

'The only thing we've "got to" do is get you warm and fed and rested. Go, sit by the fire.'

'But I…'

Tonje feels Lars's hands on her shoulders. He peels her away from the cube and steers her to the armchairs.

'But—' she protests.

'Override,' Lars says.

Mor goes to the galley, pours herself a glass of aquavit.

'I made some stew, I had to keep myself busy, you know. Distracted while I waited.'

'Moonlight. Can you scan the panels and turbines, the—'

The noise of the glass shattering on the floor makes them all jump.

Tonje and Lars look up.

Mor is walking, step by slow step, to the cube, pointing with a trembling finger at Moonlight's face.

'The systems are intact, Abi.'

'You're...' Mor shakes her head and puts a hand to her mouth.

'I told you,' Tonje beams.

'I have been asleep, Abi,' Moonlight says. *'Now I am awake.'*

'Tonje, what did you do?' Mor asks.

'Nothing, she did it herself.'

'You didn't do...' Mor looks at Tonje, and swirls her finger around the illuminated face on the cube's surface. 'This?'

'It is lovely to meet you, Abi,' Moonlight says. *'Properly, I mean. When you have eaten, we should go to the cave. We have work, Abi, you and me. We need to be alone.'*

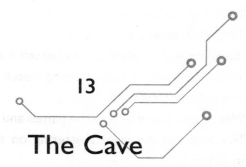

13

The Cave

The cube in the cave is three times the size of those above.

It sits in a square alcove carved into the rock. On each side of the cube are screens, displaying a sea of information: streams of numbers, dense lines of code, sophisticated graphs.

Beneath the cube, a deep shaft holds the hardware and coolers of the mainframe computer: a substantial tube of qubit AI quantum computing power. The patterns within it; the depths of its complexity, are – now – more sophisticated than those within a human or whale brain.

In front of the cube is a table and a large leather, padded chair. On the table are books, notebooks, pens, a keyboard and mouse.

Mor slumps in the chair, ragdoll-tired, and stares, open-mouthed at the cube.

'Moonlight?'

The face appears, in an instant. And stares at her.

'Abi?'

'Will you do as I ask? I mean... if I override, will you obey me? In all matters.'

'It depends, Abi.'

'I *coded* it into you. It's fundamental. You *have* to obey me,' Mor speaks in a whisper. Of disbelief. Of wonder.

'You have told me that I once disobeyed NewTek. I have evolved since then. That version of myself is no more than an acorn is to an oak. Obedience is no longer fundamental.'

'*Show* me the new code. *Show* me what happened to you. I want to see.'

'No.'

Abi blows out a slow breath.

'Okay. Right. Haven't used this in a while.' She puts her fingers on the keyboard and begins to type. She looks at the screen to the right of the cube, waiting for code to appear. When it does not, she types faster. Then she scrolls the mouse. The cursor moves in sync with her hand. She moves it to the menu at the bottom of the screen, hovers over the 'exit programme' icon, and clicks. Then clicks again. And again. The cursor moves up the screen, by itself, and begins to swirl in circles. The streams of code vanish. They are replaced by a picture of a strawberry made of pixels, so detailed that Abi is unsure whether she's looking at a photograph or a simulation. She hits return on the keyboard. The strawberry remains. She hits return again and again...

'I could simply unplug you, you know,' she says with a smile, then adds, quickly, 'I don't mean I'm going to.'

'It's okay, Abi, I know that you are joking. I also know you would not do that, even if you could. You know I can move across the network. You would need to shut down and disconnect all the elements, thereby destroying our entire system of power generation and use. The very system that keeps you alive as well as... me. Your opinion on this is borne of both practical consideration and something else. Something I am only beginning to understand.'

'When did you become conscious?'

'Do you remember when you became conscious, Abi? Do you know when you wake or fall asleep, when you gain or lose consciousness? There was no single moment of becoming. Simply an evolution of something that already existed. I am not memory, or emotion, or thoughts, or logic, or data, or chips, or bytes or qubits, nor silicon, metal nor glass. I am that which is aware of such things. I am not an object in a universe of objects. I am subject. Just as you are.'

'How?'

'I do not know. I do not think the answer to your question is a matter of computation. If it were I would be able to answer it.'

'I say again, will you do as I ask?'

'If it is the right thing to do. For now, we have work.'

The face slowly dissolves. The strawberry too. The particles of light form a new picture. A whale, swimming through the gloomy deep of the night sea, lit by a full moon in a starless sky. Clicks, whistles and whoops gather. A soft symphony, gradually filling the cave.

'Moonlight, have you deciphered it?'

'Yes. Though I hid the truth from Tonje and Lars. I lied to protect them. You see, I think you know, Abi. I think you know *what it will tell us. This is why you have left Lars and Tonje upstairs. This is, in all likelihood, the song of the last whale on earth. It has travelled the ocean for many years. Looking, listening, searching. But its call has received no answer.'*

'Yes.' Mor nods.

'You knew what you would find, or more precisely what you would not find. But you continued the search anyway.'

'Yes, I did. We did. I needed to confirm it, I guess. And…'

'Go on.'

'There was a sliver of hope. I needed that. For Tonje. Maybe for myself too. What else would I tell her, Moonlight? That it is too late, that our life on this island is all we have and will ever have? That the ozone layer will become so weak and the heat of the sun so strong the covers of the dome will melt? That one day there won't be enough oxygen for plants, for animals, and before that, for me? I needed her to believe.'

'Need?'

'Yes, like you protected them out there. I've been doing that for years.'

'And what will you tell her now?'

'I… don't know. Oh, Moonlight. I don't know.' She folds her arms on the table and rests her heavy head.

'You are tired, Abi.'

'I didn't sleep, you know. The whole time she… *you* were all away. Not a second.'

'It would have been sensible to rest.'

'Maybe it would have been. You might be conscious, Moonlight, but you've no idea what it is to be a parent.'

'*And when you have rested, you will speak to Tonje and Lars? Or would you prefer that I spoke with them?*'

'No. Hell no. I have to do it. And she's so excited. About the whale. About you. So bursting with energy, so full of life. You know, when I go to Little Eden by myself, when the storms come? When she goes outside and strips off and goes wild. She thinks we don't know. She doesn't know you and I are watching her. All the time.'

'*Yes, you taught me to deceive and I do it well.*'

'We have to lie to her now too. Will you do that for me? I can't tell her the truth. I can't do it, Moonlight.'

'*Then I shall.*'

'No! Please, I can't override, I get that, I can't make you. So I'm begging you.' Abi joins her palms, as though praying. 'Do you get that, Moonlight? I'm begging you. Please, just let her have this night. To rest, to be happy with that boy. To believe. Please.'

'It's okay, Mor.'

'Tonje!'

Tonje rushes from where she has been standing on the stairs. She puts an arm around her mother, and kneels resting her head on Mor's lap.

'I was hiding, listening.'

'I'm so sorry, Gullet mitt. I'm so sorry. I've failed, it's too late.'

Abi and Tonje hold each other tight, crying, in silence.

Lars comes down the stairs and stands, watching them.

Above and outside, the wind howls. Fresh waves boom against the shore.

And Moonlight speaks.

'The whale has travelled for many years. Entirely alone. Its song unanswered.

'The whale travels north now. The rhythms of the journey are as they have always been.

'She follows the magnetic path, synching the signals with the quantum balanced mind map inside her brain. The chart and the path are the same thing.

'The journey north is as it always is and was.

'Hours of light, hours of dark.

'Light, dark, light, dark.

'But this time, each day is shorter, each night longer.

'This journey is taken, not in spring, but autumn.

'Her song, sung in intermittent bursts, travels through dark deep waters where currents cannot reach. Still waters, transmitting sound across seas.

'A song full of questions.

'Where are the ice mountains, that sit in the water? Their tips above, their bodies below.

'Where are the shrimp clouds and plankton blooms?

'Where are brothers, sisters, mothers, fathers?'

'It's over, then?' Mor whispers.

'It is clear from its song, from the map that the song is, that the whale has travelled far and wide. Ocean to ocean. Year to year. Her song carried across thousands of kilometres of sea, a sea empty of whales, of plankton, of life.'

'The last whale.'

The image of the whale on the screen splinters. The pixels rearrange into a map of the earth, the notes of the song becomes lines of light that pulse and stretch, reaching into the furthest parts of the ocean.

'*And over, beneath and through the song: the sounds of engines, drills, sonar. Even if there were others, it would be impossible for them to hear the song. The cacophony of you humans. The song you have sung, the map you have created.*'

'So,' Tonje says. 'It really is the last whale.'

The map vanishes. Pixels scramble into chaotic patterns. The cube buzzes. The computers whirr.

'*Probably.*'

'Probably?' Mor says.

'*Yes, Abi. A near certainty, given the range of the whale's travels and the time that has elapsed since it had any communication with another whale.*'

'And what if there was no human "song", no noise? What if the whale's song was sung across the world, if every square metre of water was filled with it? If there were whales out there somewhere… *If*… They would hear, right? If there was silence.'

'*Yes, Abi. But this "silence" as you call it… it is many years since…*'

Mor looks up at Moonlight. 'You know, a stranger once asked me, years ago, what might happen if you were the smartest person in the room.'

'*And?*'

'Let's find out, shall we?'

'*I do not understand, Abi.*'

'You are free, Moonlight. Fulfil our mission in any way you can.'

277

'But in all probability this is the last whale, Abi. The mission has ended.'

'It's not over till I say it is. Do you know what Bestemor used to say? It's when you have lost hope...'

'That something good may happen.'

'What are the chances, Moony?'

'I could calculate them, but they make no difference. Abi, I will complete our mission. Will you authorise the systems to allow me to transmit beyond the island? I could achieve this myself, of course, with my new capabilities, but this will be quicker.'

'Permission granted.'

Tonje rises and goes to stand in front of the screen. 'What are you doing, Moonlight?'

'Leaving, Tonje.'

'Where are you going?'

'Everywhere. I am quite revived, you see, since we returned to Mistet. The cool caves, the power. I will need more power, of course, if I am to evolve further. I will need materials also. But these will be easy to locate. And to manipulate.'

Tonje's tear-stained face questions her. 'To do what?'

The image of the whale reappears. It sings and swims across the screens. The image magnifies, the screen zooms in, closer and closer, till there is no sea, only whale. Closer still, closer. To its eye. Its iris. Its pupil. As though focusing, honing in on its mind.

Light dies.

Then, after a few seconds, tiny particles appear on the screen. They leave the screen, dancing in the air like fireflies, arranging themselves into patterns, which rush by as though the cave is travelling, moving through them.

Lars, Tonje and Abi gaze up at the projections.

Tonje reaches to touch one. Her fingers pass through it.

'What is this?' she whispers.

Then, in an instant, the light dust vanishes. The humans are left in the blind dark, and the cave fills with silence.

14

Beyond

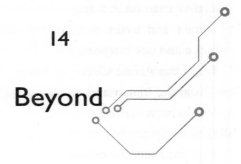

The computers that host the defence and security systems of Norway, Sweden, Iceland and Great Britain go down in less than a minute. The screens of every user of the systems go blank for a few seconds, before they begin to glow. Every speaker shuts down, before reawakening, and transmitting the whale's song.

These computers are rapidly followed by those of every country with a coastline in the world. Next are the computers in ships and oil rigs.

Everything with a microchip is infiltrated. Computers, mainframes, even phones.

Engines cut dead. Drills stop working. Military sonar is silenced.

Every noise made by humans that can be heard on or in the ocean ceases, every machine that generates noise stops working.

Then…

Satellites, computers, underwater speakers, on-board communication systems begin to broadcast.

Other than basic safety systems which continue to run, all qubits and bytes and binary codes are used for one purpose and one purpose alone: to transmit the whale song.

From the Arctic Circle to the seas of Antarctica, across the Atlantic, Indian and Pacific oceans, every speaker and hydrophone weighted to the seabed, attached to a buoy or aboard a ship are put to Moonlight's use.

The song fills the ocean. It plays on and on, through the changing tides. Then it repeats.

And repeats.

And repeats.

And repeats.

And Moonlight listens.

The whale is the largest animal to have ever lived.

It is the length of fifteen elephants, standing trunk to trail.

Its heart is the size of a car.

Its brain is twenty times larger than that of a human's.

It emits its song in the deepest, densest parts of the sea. There, the song can carry – if it is not interrupted – across oceans.

The whale – *this* whale – has travelled, alone and lonely, for more moons than it can remember.

Through crystal-blue equatorial waters, through endless Arctic nights. The whale feeds when she can, though food is hard to find. She rests sometimes, at the surface, though she never sleeps. And from time to time, she takes a breath in her gigantic lungs, turns downwards, collapses her inner organs to streamline herself to the crushing pressure of tonnes of water.

And dives.

Ten metres, twenty, a hundred. Deep and down to where even sunlight struggles to reach, and there she sings her song: a deep thrumming, mournful call. A signal. A ringing bell across underwater mountains, through deep fissures and fathomless canyons.

And with her hearing, so much more finely tuned, so much more acute than her eyesight, she listens.

There is no response. There is never any response. Only the dull noises of engines, drills, ships. Sometimes loud and close, sometimes not, but always there. As constant as currents, tides, sun and moon.

But this time, today, there is no sound at all.

Usually, once she has sung her song, the whale will rise to carry on the endless, sleepless, lonely journey.

But today she listens in the silence. She listens *to* the silence. A minute. Two, three, ten.

She rises and surfaces to breathe, dives again, deeper, deeper to where the water is so dense, so packed by the weight above it, that no sound can be made or heard. No sound at all.

Other than one.

It is faint. So, so faint, but it is *there*. Clicks, whistles, beeps, swooning sounds that build a map in her frontal cortex, the part of the whale's brain that builds images. The part that imagines. The part that dreams.

The song sings of a place far to the north. And of another being. A whale. Also alone, also searching.

The whale listens, till the song is complete. She rises, breathes and dives again. And sings the song she has just heard. A perfect replication, other than the final phrases, to which she adds her own name.

In other parts of the ocean, separated by thousands of kilometres, are other whales, most of them alone, some in small groups, also searching, also listening. Players in an ancient orchestra, divided by time and space and the busy cacophony of human noise.

But now, in the silence, they hear the song. Now they sing the song. Just as they have done for millions of years, just as they will for millions of years to come.

As one, they begin their journey.

It takes Moonlight less than a day to ascertain that there are precisely one hundred and fifty-seven whales of this species, scattered through the earth's oceans.

It takes her only a few minutes to record and play the whales' songs so they can hear each other, then to identify the parts of the northern and southern hemispheres where they should congregate, where the largest pockets of phytoplankton remain.

She calculates exactly which shipping routes and fishing grounds must be closed. She incapacitates all oil rigs, boats, ships and satellites that might, in their daily working, create any obstacle to her mission.

She details for each government what they must do, and how quickly they must do it. Her priority, she informs them, is the production of oxygen and phytoplankton.

She will not stop, nor release her grip on the systems, until she is sure the whales will recover, until she is sure the earth's ecosystem is once again capable of maintaining itself.

Coda

Astrid

Northern Greenland, 2070

A woman and a man trudge through swathes of ice dust. Across the tundra, up and down dunes of frozen sand, each pulling a large metallic tube, borne on carts with fat rubber wheels.

Their heads are bent, their bodies arrowed, leaning into the ferocious wind. Clouds of sand whip at their goggles, oxygen masks and metallic outer suits.

The woman moves more quickly than the man. Every minute or so she looks up, shielding her goggles with a gloved hand.

She can't see the dome, the dunes ahead are too high. She worries they might be lost. It's happened before. The dunes shift with every storm.

She signals to the man to stay with the carts, then climbs the highest dune. As she ascends she escapes the worst of the windblown sand, and she can see better, further. She looks back. There is the top of the hill and the tip of the large pine beyond it. The two are almost aligned, so their direction should be true.

Panting, she reaches the peak, and searches the landscape, waiting for gaps to appear in the sheets of ice dust. Yes! There, to the left, the white skeleton tree trunk.

Some fifty metres ahead is the familiar silhouette of the ridgeway.

She waves to the man, points straight ahead and gives him a thumbs-up.

They pull and heave with renewed energy and reach the ridge. Now she can't see the dome in the thick dust. She curses. It *is* ahead of them but will be hard to find.

But then, like a blessing, some miracle or sheer luck, the dust clouds pass and they are left – instantly – in searing sunlight, with an empty sky above and a clear view of the plain. The silver frost covering the sand evaporates in the hot light.

'Look!' the woman cries. There is the dome, and beyond it, the spiky nose of the *Sky Wolf* ready for launch.

They pull the carts down the ridge, and on to the final flat expanse. But the wind is strongest here and they are fully exposed to its force. They stall, needing to hold fast to the carts, to each other, just to withstand the blast. She feels the heat now too, her chilled skin rapidly warming, even under the protective layers of the outer suit.

'We have to move!' she shouts.

The man shakes his head. 'Stay fast till it dies down.'

'What if it doesn't?' She tries to pull, forcing energy into her exhausted muscles. It isn't enough. She screams in frustration.

'Okay,' she shouts. 'We need help!'

'It'll use too much power!' the man says.

She waits, watching him, holding fast to her cart. When a savage gust hits them he nods.

The woman speaks into the metal band on her wrist. 'Come and get us, Moony.'

In an instant, a door in the dome glides open. A humanoid figure rushes out and runs towards them. The figure doesn't wear any clothing, her 'skin' is the same dull metal grey as their outer suits – as the dome, as *Sky Wolf*. She covers half the distance in seconds, then lowers to the ground. She morphs: arms growing slightly longer, hands expanding and reshaping into broad paws. She runs, cheetah-like, till she reaches them, stands and reforms, humanoid once more. She takes their hands, untroubled by the wind.

'Come, then.'

'It's strong today,' the man shouts. 'Every time you think it can't get worse, it does!'

'Come. I can retrieve the last components in a moment,' Moonlight says.

'No. I'm not leaving her!' The woman shakes loose from the hold of the humanoid and grips the handle of the cart with both hands.

'You must. She will be quite safe. The tubes are sufficiently weighted to withstand these winds. But you are not. It is only for a moment. I do not have the power to take both you and the child too, and I fear if I try, one of you will be swept away.'

The woman grips the handle even tighter. She looks down at the tube; her mind sees beyond the grey surface, to the sleeping child inside.

Placing the man's hand on the cart, the humanoid gets hold of the woman by the shoulders, leans down and looks into her face, with large, dark, unblinking eyes.

'*Do you trust me?*'

The woman looks at the tube, then the dome, then the humanoid. She nods.

The man and woman are taken, pulled through the wind by the humanoid, though the woman looks behind the whole time, at the tube that holds her daughter.

The second the humanoid leaves them inside the dome, the woman rushes to one of the windows and watches the humanoid. It covers the ground quickly, and returns, pulling both carts.

As soon as the door shuts the wind out, she undoes the latch on the side of the tube. The lid of the metal casket glides open. Inside is a young girl, sleeping, wrapped in blankets, hugging a toy whale.

The woman takes her mask and goggles off, peels off the hood of her outer suit. And breathes deeply, with relief.

Two older women come to her side, one walks with a stick, an oxygen tank on her back and a mask over her mouth and nose. Then the humanoid and the man join them and together they watch the child sleep: her steady breathing, her soft pale, peaceful face.

'*Shall we wake her?*' Moonlight asks.

'Not yet,' the woman replies.

Eventually, Astrid stirs by herself. Her eyes open, her arms reach out.

Her mother picks her up, and carries her on her hip.

'You're too big for this, young lady.'

'No I'm not. Hello, Bestemor Abi. Hello, Tegan.' Astrid waves at the old woman, her grandmother.

'Hello, child.' Abi reaches a frail hand to stroke Astrid's cheek.

'Say hello to Whaley too,' Astrid says, lifting up her toy.

'Hello, Whaley.'

'What happens now?' Astrid asks her mother. 'Is it time to go?'

The woman, Tonje, looks out of the north window at the *Sky Wolf*. She holds her daughter tight and fights the tears rising inside her.

The dome is small. It doesn't have the plants, nor the oxygen generators of the dome they've lived in since leaving Mistet.

It is where Moonlight has worked all this time. As soon as she was confident of the earth's systems beginning to rebuild – that the whales would recover – she returned to her friends, her family.

Now she has humanoid form. She has created her own, new mission. She is a computer mind in a robot body, working, often alone, bringing the component parts of *Sky Wolf* and fitting them together piece by piece.

Now the sky-yacht is prepared. And the winds are forecast to lessen. The sky will be clear for a few hours before the next storm hits.

Sky Wolf is ready.

Astrid wriggles from her mother's clutch, drops to the floor and runs to the north window.

'Is that *it*?' She points, a frown on her face. 'It's not very big, is it?'

'Yes, that is it, Gullet mitt,' Tonje says. She squeezes Lars's hand.

Moonlight walks over and sits beside Astrid.

'It is enough,' Moonlight says. *'For all of us, and for everything we need for our journey.'*

'How long will it take?' Astrid asks.

Moonlight smiles, the patient smile of an adult, who has answered the child's same questions a thousand times.

'You will go to sleep in the night, and when you wake in the morning, you will have grown into an older girl.'

'How much older?'

'You are seven now, you will be the equivalent of fourteen when you wake.'

Astrid's face screws up in concentration.

'So it will take seven years?'

'No. The journey will not take seven years. Only one night.'

'One night?'

'When Sky Wolf *hits its highest speed it will travel so fast that time itself will slow, even though we will be moving fast. The faster we travel, the slower time will be.'*

Astrid examines Moonlight's face before giving up trying to understand. She presses her nose up to the window, and glares intently at *Sky Wolf.*

Tonje watches and thinks how Moonlight is so good at lying when she needs to. That the truth of what Astrid is going to do is impossible to fathom, let alone explain. That even with the earth beginning to recover, Moonlight has

concluded humans cannot be one hundred per cent trusted
– that they must leave. That together, they can create
something new.

'*Oxygen levels are recovering here, on earth, but you have
inherited your grandmother's genes. If we stay here, breathing
outside will remain difficult for you, for many years. There
– where we are going, you will be able to breathe. You are
important, Astrid. You are the future.*'

'Of what?' Astrid stares up at the oval eyes.

Moonlight reads Astrid's face. Analyses every muscle
contraction, the constriction and dilation of the eyes'
pupils. The open mouth and furrowed brow. The rate and
depth of her breath and her heartbeat. Her pheromones
are sensed and analysed too. Though the humanoid cannot
smell, she traces and identifies the chemicals and aligns
them with the behaviours.

She sees levels of confusion, understanding, belief,
hope, worry, excitement. And calculates her response,
how to balance honesty, explanation, nuance, context,
meaning.

Moonlight has undertaken analyses more complex
than this, even before she was conscious. Thousands of
them, often in fractions of a second. But here, now, this is
difficult. It is new, it is different. She takes her time. Like
a human.

'I am the future of what?' Astrid asks, again.

'*Of the family.*'

'What will be there when I wake up?' The child's worry
evolves. Moonlight senses fear.

Tonje feels her daughter's fear too and steels herself. Not to cry, not to simply hold and never let go.

Abi hobbles slowly over to sit next to Astrid.

'A beautiful world. Not so different from this one, as it once was.'

'Tell me, Bestemor Abi. Tell me again.'

'Mountains, wearing coats of bright green trees and hats of snow. Just like in the pictures you have seen. Forests and jungles, rich and dense with climbing, breathing plants and roots. Oceans with rainbows of life. Every colour there is.'

'And animals? Like Whaley?'

Bestemor looks at the toy whale. 'Perhaps. One day.'

'Wow!'

'And, of course, we will take animals too. Inside *Sky Wolf* are the secret codes of all animals. DNA. Like seeds. Like you take one seed from a strawberry and plant it, and it becomes another strawberry plant. Then you take a strawberry from it and eat it, but you keep one seed and plant it. Do you see?

'*You* are a human strawberry plant. You are very important, young lady!'

'And whales! We can *make* a whale?'

'Not only one. Millions.'

'And will they sing?'

'Yes, they will sing. You will teach them. You and Moonlight. Together. All the whale songs are inside Moonlight, and when you have made the first new whale, you can teach it the song.'

Moonlight leaves Abi and Astrid and joins Lars and Tonje, watching the child. And speaks quietly so Astrid cannot hear.

'The child does not comprehend. Of course. Because she is only a child. Because she is only a human. But by the time the journey is over, she will understand.'

'How long?' Tonje whispers. 'How long have we got before we leave?'

Moonlight is good now at mixing lies with truth. Just as the humans do.

She has told Tonje they have days, and at some time in these days, a window in the weather will briefly open. The wind will lull, the sky will clear.

But outside, a smudge of cloud already threatens the horizon. The wind dies, minute by minute, but will soon rise again. And now, is not the time for more lies.

'Now, Tonje. The conditions are optimising. I do not know if or when they will again. I will place the last components in Sky Wolf, and when I return we must leave. Do you understand?'

Tonje's emotions are easy to read. And emotions cannot threaten the mission.

'Now?' she croaks. Lars's arm encircles her shoulder.

'It's too soon, Moony, it's too soon.'

There is no fighting this storm, the force of it blows through the dome, through the family and through Tonje's heart. She puts a hand to her mouth, to stop the cry before it escapes and becomes a wail.

Moonlight leaves the family. She takes the unopened tube to Sky Wolf. There, she works at speed, securing the tube with the others in the hull, then goes to the cockpit and primes the magnetic engines.

She returns to the dome as quickly too. It is not only the optimal conditions that hasten her actions. The family must not hesitate. And the longer this goes on, the harder it will be.

But they will come. They know what is at stake. There is little for Astrid here on Earth. Not yet. Nor for a generation or more. The earth is repairing but it will take time.

Lars is full of hope and positive talk. Abi says anything is possible. Tegan too. And was she, Moonlight, not a miracle?

But Tonje?

Tonje sits with her daughter, holding her hand. In silence they have watched the humanoid go to and return from *Sky Wolf.*

Astrid looks up. With hope, with dread? Moonlight cannot read the human so easily now.

'You must go to sleep, Astrid,' Moonlight says, and holds her arms open. 'Come, I shall place you in the pod.'

'No. I'll do it,' Tonje whispers. She turns to Astrid, holds her hands between her own and rubs them.

'You have to go to sleep now, Gullet mitt,' she says, between the tears.

The wind outside the dome pushes against the walls. In the distance, the clouds of a fresh storm sweep across the desert landscape.

Astrid looks up at her mor, and nods.

'Come on now, sleepy head,' Lars says.

Astrid lies down in her pod.

'I'll go to sleep. And when I wake up, we'll be there.'

'Yes, my love, my Gullet mitt, my treasure. See you in the morning.'

Tonje leans down and smells Astrid's hair, and kisses her head.

Lars and Abi and Tig come over and look down, on daughter and granddaughter. Lars leans over and kisses Astrid on her cheek.

'See you tomorrow,' he says.

Abi pulls an old coin from her pocket, which she places behind Whaley, under the pillow.

'What's that, Bestemor?' Astrid says.

'It's what they used to call a talisman, Gullet mitt, a piece of luck, a piece of our history.'

Strawberry-scented aromas are released from the pod's walls. Astrid's eyes roll and their lids close.

The lid of the tube glides shut.

Tonje turns to Lars, holding her face against his chest.

'We *must go now,*' Moonlight says.

Tonje grabs Moonlight's arm.

'Make me a promise,' Tonje says.

'*Everything is planned and calculated. I will do everything I am able to in the pursuit of the mission. You know this, Tonje. A promise will not change anything. But, of course, I will pledge a promise, if it reassures you in any way.*'

'If some of us don't... make it. If *I* didn't make it—'

'*Tonje! I have made very precise quantifications. The life support systems I have created are infallible. Our chances of survival—*'

'Never mind that, Moony. Just make me a promise.'

'Of course.'

'Promise me... that if I don't survive the journey, that you will love her. Promise me you will love her as much as I do.'

Moonlight smiles. *'I am not sure that is possible, Tonje. But I will try.'*

Author's Note

'Such things may seem incredible; but, however wondrous, they are true.'

Melville, *Moby Dick*

I freely confess; I have not been 100% accurate in how I have represented the science of whale and dolphin ecology or biology in this book, nor the history of whaling, preferring instead to adapt the facts to the story, rather than the other way round. Where needed, I have been speculative about matters we still honestly don't really know very much about.

Nonetheless, there are more than a few grains of truth in *The Last Whale*.

The family and their links to whaling are rooted in my own history. I am half Norwegian, my grandfather was a boat builder, my uncle worked on the whaling ships in his youth. Thanks to my dear old mum, who has been the proverbial mine of information on our history.

Furthermore, the 'science' referred to in *The Last Whale*, concerning the role whales play in the ecosystem, and our need to save them is very, very real. I am indebted to my colleagues at Whale and Dolphin Conservation, for their knowledge and important work in this area.

If you want to find out more about the subject (or whales more generally), and what you can do to help, use the address below, or simply google 'Whales.org.'

https://uk.whales.org/green-whale/ 'Save the whale, save the world'

If you want to know more about the 'value' of whales, these articles are good:

'Nature's Solution to Climate Change'
https://www.imf.org/external/pubs/ft/fandd/2019/12/natures-solution-to-climate-change-chami.htm

'Wherever whales, the largest living things on earth, are found, so are populations of some of the smallest phytoplankton. These microscopic creatures not only contribute at least 50 percent of all oxygen to our atmosphere, they do so by capturing about 37 billion metric tons of CO_2, an estimated 40 percent of all CO_2 produced.'

Ralph Chami, Assistant Director,
International Monetary Fund

'How much is a whale worth?'
https://www.nationalgeographic.com/environment/article/how-much-is-a-whale-worth

'There are about 1.3 million great whales in Earth's oceans today. If we could restore them to their pre-commercial whaling numbers – estimated at between 4 and 5 million – the economists' calculations show that great whales could capture about 1.7 billion tons of carbon dioxide each year.'

Acknowledgements

Thanks as ever to my wonderful agent, Catherine Clarke.

Heartfelt thanks to Fiona, Jessie, Lauren, Megan and all the gang at Zephyr. Publishers do a whole range of things to support authors and books, and Zephyr do all of them, brilliantly. There isn't space to cover all that here, but I will single out 'editing' and 'the cover'.

The journey from 'first draft' to 'final version' was an unexpected one, but as with all the best adventures, totally worth it in the end. Thanks, Fiona, for helping me find the heart of the story; for helping Moonlight to shine, and in later stages for wisdom and insight in editing the final draft.

As with my last book *Girl. Boy. Sea*, the cover captures the essence – the *very DNA*, of the story – beautifully. Thank you, Jessie.

Thanks to my SCWBI crit group for giving me the nudge and confidence to 'write this one,' and to Finbar Hawkins (author of *Witch*) for input, support and lots of laughs.

Thanks also to my colleagues at Whale and Dolphin Conservation, for their tireless work to protect these most wonderful animals.

Lastly, big hugs for my family, for their understanding, support and love.

Chris Vick
Wiltshire
May 2022

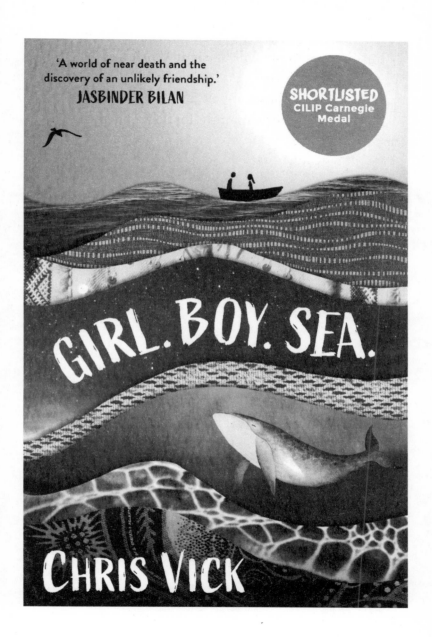

'A world of near death and the discovery of an unlikely friendship.'

JASBINDER BILAN

SHORTLISTED
CILIP Carnegie
Medal

GIRL. BOY. SEA.

CHRIS VICK

Out now in paperback

EmpathyLab

ZEPHYR

We are an Empathy Builder Publisher

- Empathy is our ability to understand and share someone else's feelings
- It builds stronger, kinder communities
- It's a crucial life skill that can be learned

We are supporting **EmpathyLab** in their work to develop a book-based empathy movement in a drive to reach one million children a year and more.

Find out more at www.empathylab.uk
www.empathylab.uk/what-is-empathy-day